BBC

DOCTOR WHO

The Stone Rose

The Doctor Who *History Collection*

The Stone Rose
Jacqueline Rayner

The Roundheads
Mark Gatiss

The Witch Hunters
Steve Lyons

Dead of Winter
James Goss

Human Nature
Paul Cornell

The English Way of Death
Gareth Roberts

The Shadow in the Glass
Justin Richards and Stephen Cole

Amorality Tale
David Bishop

THE HISTORY COLLECTION EDITION

THE STONE ROSE

JACQUELINE RAYNER

1 2 3 4 5 6 7 8 9 10

BBC Books, an imprint of Ebury Publishing
20 Vauxhall Bridge Road, London SW1V 2SA

BBC Books is part of the Penguin Random House group of companies whose addresses can be found at global.penguinrandomhouse.com

This book is published to accompany the television series entitled *Doctor Who*, broadcast on BBC One. *Doctor Who* is a BBC Wales production.
Executive producers: Steven Moffat and Brian Minchin

This edition published in 2015 by BBC Books, an imprint of Ebury Publishing.
First published in 2006 by BBC Worldwide Ltd.

www.eburypublishing.co.uk

A CIP catalogue record for this book is available from the British Library

ISBN 978 1 849 90906 8

Editorial director: Albert DePetrillo
Series consultant: Justin Richards
Project editor: Steve Tribe
Cover design: Two Associates © Woodlands Books Ltd, 2015
Production: Alex Goddard

Printed and bound in the USA

INTRODUCTION

For the first set of New Series novels, Steve Cole, Justin Richards and I had to write for the Ninth Doctor before we'd actually seen him on telly. That was tricky. 'At least we won't have to do something like that again for a while,' I remember at least one of us saying. Ha! Little did we know that Christopher Eccleston's departure from the role would be announced before those initial three books had even hit the shelves. So there we were in 2005, poring over David Tennant's back catalogue (not a hardship), trying to commit to the page a Doctor we knew very little about (that Children in Need special in November was a godsend). At least we knew Rose! (I loved Rose.)

Back then, the books were made in sets of three: one past, one present, one future. For the initial Ninth Doctor books I'd been assigned the present-day one. This time I was given the historical – or rather, as pure historicals weren't allowed, the pseudo-historical. I'd spent three years studying Roman history at university, so I decided to finally put my degree to good use and set the story there. *The Stone Rose* is quite unusual for me in that I can trace several of the ideas in it to specific influences. (Normally the 'where do you get your ideas from?' chest is bare. I have (literally) no idea!) As a child, I frequently borrowed a particular book of short stories from the library. One story was about a little girl who lived in a jungle with many animal friends, and the local sorcerer would announce that he needed a particular item for his home – say, a fan – then he'd invite the parrot to tea, and the next day no one would be able to find the parrot but the man would have a beautiful feathered fan on the wall of his house. The end of the story came when the man announced he wanted a little black stool for his house and invited the girl to tea, but she was clever and swapped the cups and the evil man turned into a (big, white) stool instead. I've never been able to track down the book – not entirely surprising, I guess, as all I can remember about it is that it had a pink cover, and if you do a google search for 'little black stool' and 'parrot' all you get is stuff about very unpleasant bird illnesses – but the story has stayed with me. It's not just the evil of someone killing a fellow creature, it's that they turn them into a *thing*, a final indignity. (There's a Dorothy L. Sayers story, *The Abominable History of the Man with Copper Fingers*, that also deals with people being turned into art, which sends shudders down my spine.) So, that was where Ursus's unpleasant skill came from.

Then there was the GENIE. That had its roots in another short story that haunted me, although one that's considerably more well known – *The Monkey's Paw* by W.W. Jacobs. Just in case you're not familiar with it, it's the tale of a couple who come into possession of a monkey's paw that grants three wishes. With their first wish, they ask for a sum of money – after which their only son is killed, and that exact sum given to them as compensation. Then the wife wants to use the paw to wish for their son to return to life. The husband protests – not only has the boy been dead ten days, but he was hideously mutilated in the fatal accident – but eventually gives in. That night something comes knocking at their door, but the husband uses the final wish to wish it gone before they see what's awaiting them… It's a very simple story, but oh so terrifying. Wishes are scary things, if you take them literally. I actually found that in *The Stone Rose* I had to tone down Rose's wishes to stop it becoming full-on horror and keep it suitable for younger readers.

What else can I tell you about the book? My visual memory is appalling, and I absolutely hate having to create and describe imaginary places. One way around this is to base the setting on a real place. In this case I went one step further and set part of the book actually in a real place: the British Museum. So one day I went along to the British Museum and wrote down everything I saw. The only part of the book's museum that wasn't in the real museum was the statue of Rose itself, but I'd decided exactly where it would be placed, between two statues that were really there. I had some lovely letters from people who said they'd visited the museum and found the place where the statue was supposed to have stood, which made me very happy.

Oh, readers' letters! When I was growing up, I knew one other female *Doctor Who* fan. At university, it was pretty much just me. As I found my way into *Doctor Who* fandom I met others, and though there was a definite female presence we were still very much a minority. Then the new series came along, and suddenly girls *loved* it. I found the proof of that in the letters I received when *The Stone Rose* was published. Ninety per cent were from girls, and ninety per cent of that ninety per cent were talking about one tiny bit of the story. The bit where the Doctor actually *kissed* Rose. Oh, it may have been just an act of supreme *joie de vivre,* but it was still *kissing*. Probably just as many people hated that bit as loved it, they just didn't write to tell me, but it was interesting to find out what this new audience was particularly keen on. Having discovered this, I suggested taking it further and planned a whole series of adventures* wherein the First Doctor planted a smacker on Dodo's lips, the Seventh Doctor had a bit of a smooch with Mel etc. etc., but for some reason the BBC didn't want to go for it. So here you go, the first and only entry in my 'Kissing Companions' series: *The Stone Rose.*

Jacqueline Rayner
September 2014

* This is a lie.

For Debbie, who made the Roman years so much fun

Rose carefully dropped three pound coins into the large collecting box at the entrance to the British Museum.

Her mum tutted. 'What d'you want to go and do that for? You don't have to pay.'

'It's a donation,' Rose pointed out. 'They suggest you make one.'

Jackie raised disbelieving eyes towards the huge domed ceiling. 'That's only for people who haven't been dragged here against their wills on a Sunday morning.'

Rose laughed and exchanged a look with Mickey. 'You didn't have to come, Mum.'

Jackie tossed back her long blonde hair. 'You think I was going to stay behind? It's a surprise, Mickey said. Come and see, Mickey said. You'll never believe it. Mind you, things I've seen, can't imagine what I'm not going to believe, but—'

'You're right,' Rose interrupted. 'I didn't really expect you to stay behind. Come on. Let's get on with it, then.'

As Mickey moved off, Rose looked around for the fourth member of their party, but the Doctor had already vanished into one of the galleries. Shrugging, she walked off anyway, following Mickey's lead.

Mickey had been really excited to see her this time – even more than usual. Because he had a surprise for her. A huge surprise. An unbelievable surprise. And they were on their way to see it.

They passed the marble lion that gazed on the museum's Great Court with hollow, sorrowful eyes.

'He looks so sad,' Rose said.

'You'd be miserable if you'd been stuck in a museum for –' Jackie bent down to read the little plaque beneath the statue – 'nearly two and a half thousand years.'

Rose didn't point out that the museum hadn't been around for anywhere near that long, because she knew her mum knew it anyway. But she understood what Jackie meant. She had a sudden wave of illogical pity for the carved creature, frozen for ever due to a sculptor's whim over two millennia ago.

Jackie was still looking at the lion. 'Two and a half thousand years,' she said again. 'That's even older than him.'

'Him', Rose knew, was the Doctor.

'Hey, why doesn't he get wrinkles? I mean, however many hundred years, even with the new body, got to do something to the skin. Free radicals and all that. I bet we're not the only planet with pollution. Can you find out what he uses? Make a fortune, he could.'

'This is the Doctor we're talking about, not Dad.' Rose rolled her eyes. 'He's no salesman.'

Mickey was beckoning them, and they left the statue and headed on. There was the Doctor in the Egyptian gallery, examining the Rosetta Stone.

'It was a right pain when they found this,' he said, giving a little wave as they passed. 'There I was, just about to launch my English-hieroglyphic dictionary, when along come Napoleon's soldiers and the bottom falls out of the market.'

'There. Not a salesman,' Rose said. 'Told you.' She waved back, then they headed down a flight of steps and round a corner, Mickey never hesitating, as if he knew the way by heart.

They passed rows of carved Roman heads, hundreds of sightless eyes watching their progress. Then there were some sarcophagi, and a giant stone foot that seemed almost too comedic to be in such a serious place as a museum.

Then they came to a row of statues, sculpted human forms, some headless, some armless, but all possessed of a shining white dignity despite their misfortunes.

Mickey stopped. 'There you are,' he said. He was grinning, a dog who'd just fetched her a stick and was waiting for a grateful response.

Rose looked at the statue in front of her, a marble priestess with a veil. It was lovely, but not all that exciting.

Then Jackie gasped. 'Oh, my God. I don't believe it!'

Rose transferred her gaze to the next sculpture along. And she gasped too.

It was a perfect stone replica – of herself.

And, according to its sign, it was nearly 2,000 years old.

ONE

Once Rose had recovered from the initial shock of finding a statue of herself in the British Museum, she got quite excited. 'That's brilliant!' she said. 'D'you realise what this means? We must be off to –' she checked – 'second-century Rome. How brilliant is that?'

'Blimey,' said a voice from behind. 'Reminds me of a girl I once knew. Wonder whatever happened to her.' The Doctor had caught up with them and he gave Rose a smile that could probably melt even a marble statue. She grinned at him.

Jackie was reading the sign under the sculpture. 'Here, it says it's a statue of the goddess Fortuna,' she said. 'Don't tell me I've given birth to a god. Howard'll never believe it.'

'Fortuna, Roman goddess of good luck,' the Doctor told her. 'Portrayed with a cornucopia.'

'Says here it's a horn of plenty,' said Jackie.

The Doctor looked amused.

The Rose figure was indeed cradling a cornucopia, overflowing with stone fruit and flowers, in the crook of one arm. The other arm was no longer whole, a wrist stump gesturing redundantly at the group gathered round it. Rose held up her own two hands. 'I hope that wasn't done from life,' she said.

'Tell you what, though,' said Jackie, 'she's wearing your earrings.'

Rose took off one to compare. It was a flat silver disc with a spiral pattern radiating out from a tiny flower in the centre. She held it up by the statue's ear. Identical, even down to the flower. 'That's incredible,' she said. 'It's so detailed.' She slipped the real earring into the pocket of her denim jacket and grinned. 'Looks like I've got a future ahead of me as an artist's model! I've always fancied that.'

Mickey frowned. 'When my mate Vic asked you to pose for him, you said no.'

Rose sighed. 'Yeah, but lying on a sheepskin rug in my undies while your mate Vic takes photos isn't quite the same as posing as a goddess for some ancient Roman.'

The Doctor had put on his glasses and was examining the statue's remaining hand. 'Hmm,' he said.

'What's up?' Rose asked.

'Statue's wearing your ring too.'

Rose looked down at the ring on her right hand. 'If she's wearing my earrings, why not?'

The Doctor frowned. 'They often made the torsos separately – mass-produced them, then just stuck on a head. Obviously the sculptor was so enamoured of your figure that you got to be the model for the whole thing.'

'And is that so hard to understand?' asked Rose, raising an eyebrow.

The Doctor swung round and gave her a disarming grin. 'I'm sure it isn't.'

Rose found it quite hard to tear herself away from her stone double, but as the Doctor pointed out, if she stayed there looking at it for ever, then it would never get made and they'd all be swallowed up in a terrible paradox. So she let herself be led away, past the giant foot – 'Ah, my fault,' the Doctor commented. 'The last remains of the Ogre of Hyfor Three. Silicon-based life form. I defeated it back in, oh, must be AD two hundred and something. There was me: take that, you evil ogre! And there was it: ha, ha, you'll never defeat me! And there was me: don't be so sure about that...'

'It says it's from a colossal acrolithic statue,' Mickey pointed out hurriedly.

'Well, they would say that,' said the Doctor – past the sarcophagi, past the rows of stone heads, their gazes now seeming to signify kinship to Rose.

They lost the Doctor in the Egyptian section again, and Jackie went off to see if she could find a postcard of her stone daughter. Rose and Mickey stood together in the entrance, waiting.

'So, how d'you find out about it?' asked Rose after a few moments' silence. 'Not your usual haunt, this, is it?'

Mickey seemed embarrassed, looking down at the floor.

She opened her eyes wide. 'What? It can't be that bad, can it? You've not been robbin' it or something? Or you been seeing one of the girls in the gift shop and you don't wanna tell me about it?'

He frowned a no, but still looked sheepish.

'Come on. Tell me!' she said.

Mickey put back his shoulders, attempting a bit of bravado. 'Well... I've been doing this volunteer stuff. You know, kids and that.'

Rose laughed delightedly. 'But that's brilliant!'

He shrugged, embarrassed again. 'Well, there's you off

doing good all round the universe – just thought I'd do a bit at home, that's all.'

The Doctor was approaching them now. 'Don't tell him,' Mickey hissed.

Rose sighed, exasperated. 'Yeah, 'cause being a nice person's *so* uncool, isn't it?' But she couldn't help reaching up and giving Mickey a quick peck on the cheek. 'You old softy.'

Jackie joined them, her postcard hunt having proved unsuccessful, and the four of them made their way out into the sunshine.

'Well, bye for now. Take care. Don't do anything I wouldn't,' said the Doctor as they reached the bottom of the museum's wide stone steps, holding out a hand to Mickey.

'What, you off already? Barely give me time to say hello to my only daughter before you're dragging her away again!' complained Jackie, hands on hips.

'We'd love to stay,' said the Doctor insincerely, putting a hand on Rose's shoulder. 'Love to. Love to. Love love love to. But I'm afraid we have a date to keep.'

'We have?' said Rose.

'Would have thought that was obvious,' said the Doctor. 'You and me are off to ancient Rome.'

'Hang on!' Jackie called after them. 'I've seen that *Rome* on telly! You just watch yourself, my girl. The things they get up to.'

Rose laughed. 'Keep your toga on, Mum! I can look after myself.'

Rose stumbled into the control room as the TARDIS lurched to one side. The Doctor was dashing round the giant bronze mushroom in the centre, pushing a button here, pulling a lever there, doing something energetic with a pump somewhere else.

She took a hesitant step forward as the time machine seemed to settle down – but it must have been waiting for that, because the instant she moved it lurched the other way. The bed sheet that had been draped over her shoulder fell to the floor, but it at least broke her fall as the next TARDIS tremor came.

'We'll be able to find somewhere to stay,' the Doctor said, looking down at her from his still-upright but fairly precarious position. 'No need to bring your own bedding.'

'It's for wearing, not sleeping,' said Rose. She sighed. 'I went to a toga party once, but I can't remember how to tie this thing around me.'

The Doctor grinned. 'Nice girls don't wear togas,' he told her.

'They don't?'

'Nope. And even if they did, they probably wouldn't have one with Winnie the Pooh on.'

Rose looked more closely at the sheet. In one corner, Winnie the Pooh sat eating honey, Piglet by his side. 'I didn't notice,' she said. 'But nice sheets you keep. You know, if any toddlers happen to come on board. So what should I wear, then, O Roman god of fashion?'

He waved a hand. 'Oh, there'll be something back there. Look under R for Rome. Or A for ancient.'

'And what about you?' she asked. 'C for conspicuous?'

The Doctor was dressed in a resolutely twenty-first-century suit with blue shirt and plimsolls, not the sort of thing that would blend in several millennia ago.

'I'll find something,' he said, leaning over to twist a dial.

The TARDIS spun too as Rose tripped towards the doorway, dragging the sheet behind her. 'It'd be a lot easier if you fixed some stabilisers to this thing,' she called back.

'Sailors keep their feet through worse than this!' he retorted happily, performing a few steps of a hornpipe to prove his point.

Rose groaned. 'Yeah, well, I couldn't half do with a tot of rum myself.' She staggered off again.

The TARDIS finally landed. Rose was now wearing an ankle-length dress in pale blue – clashing slightly with the greenness of her still-nauseous face – with a dark blue shawl draped over her head, hiding hair that was now elaborately curled and scraped off her face. The Doctor wore a plain white tunic that ended at the knees, his sonic screwdriver stuck absurdly in his belt.

'Let's hope we are in ancient Rome,' said Rose. 'You'll get lynched if you hang round the estate dressed like that.'

'I'm sure you'd rescue me,' said the Doctor.

He opened the doors and they stepped out – that first step into an alien world or time that never lost its excitement, however many times they did it.

They were in a town or city, tenement blocks to either side of them. The sky was blue, but the colder sort of blue that said spring or early autumn.

The Doctor peered up at the skyline. 'Aha! See that?' He indicated an enormous pillar with the figure of a man on top, just visible above the roofs. 'Trajan's Column. Definitely Rome, then. Unless your estate's gone majorly up in the world.'

'It stinks like the estate,' said Rose, wrinkling her nose. She took a step forward and grimaced as her sandals splashed into a deep puddle. 'And look at these streets – they're flooded! Is this Rome or Venice?'

The Doctor looked down at her feet and raised an eyebrow. 'Well, that explains the stink anyway.'

Rose frowned. 'What do you—' Then she realised. 'Oh, ugh. Ugh ugh ugh. Hey, I thought the Romans invented sewers and drains and stuff?'

'Pretty much,' the Doctor told her. 'But I don't think we've landed in the nicest part of town…'

'I'll say we haven't!' exclaimed Rose, as a cry suddenly rang out from a nearby street.

Both of them immediately began running towards the sound.

Three young men were crowded round an elderly bearded man with grey hair. He lay on the ground, clearly winded, staring up in fear at the dagger that was being waved in his face.

'Oi!' yelled Rose. 'Leave him alone!'

The men didn't even turn to look at her.

'Help!' croaked the old man. 'Please, help me!'

'Just hand over your cash, grandad. You do what we say and everything'll be fine,' said the man with the dagger.

'Er, excuse me, gentlemen,' began the Doctor confidently, striding forwards.

This time they turned to look, and Rose took advantage of the distraction. There was a pile of large clay jars in the doorway next to her and one soon found itself hurtling towards the head of the dagger-wielding mugger. The Doctor stepped in and relieved the dazed man of his weapon, as more jars connected with his two companions. Soon all three were racing off down the street, shards of pottery clinging to their hair and clothes.

'Ha!' Rose called after them, as the Doctor helped the old man to his feet. He seemed a bit shaken – well, that was hardly surprising.

'Thank you so much,' he said weakly. 'Gnaeus Fabius Gracilis at your service.'

Further introductions were put on hold as a nearby door slammed open. An angry-looking red-faced man glared down at the depleted pile of pottery at his feet. 'Here! What've you done to my amphorae?'

'Er – it was them!' Rose said mendaciously, pointing after the three muggers.

The man started after them, yelling 'Oi! Oi! Oi!' as the Doctor and Rose beat a hasty retreat in the opposite direction, carrying Gracilis between them.

'You all right?' Rose asked him, as they reached a safe distance and came to a stop. 'Did those blokes nick anything?'

The man shook his head – but the effort seemed to make him lose his balance.

The Doctor stepped in and caught him. 'Whoops! Steady there. I don't think you are all right, are you? Are you hurt?'

'No, no,' said Gracilis. 'Just the worry, you know… And I must confess I feel slightly dizzy.'

The Doctor frowned. 'Really? Can you remember what day it is?'

'Ah, I am not so weak as all that,' said the man. 'It is the Ides of March.'

Rose nearly choked. 'You're joking!'

Gracilis looked startled. 'Am I, then, wrong? Am I suffering from fever of the brain?'

The Doctor frowned at Rose but gave Gracilis a great

big reassuring smile. 'No, no, quite right. I'm assuming you know what year it is as well, though?'

'The year?' said the man incredulously. 'Of course I do. Really, sir, I appreciate your concern, and of course your brave intervention, but I assure you I am fine. There is no need for this.'

'Absolutely! You're fine,' said the Doctor, slapping Gracilis on the back and grimacing at Rose. He mouthed 'Worth a try' and then 'I'll work it out later' to her. 'Well, clean bill of health on the memory front. Excellent. But tell me, when did you last have anything to eat?'

Gracilis looked thoughtful. 'Do you know, I have no idea. Yesterday perhaps. Or possibly the day before.'

'Then before you do anything else, a bite to eat and a sit-down are on the menu. Come on.'

'But hadn't we better *beware?*' said Rose happily. 'You know, of, er, food poisoning…'

The Doctor frowned again.

'All right. Let's go get something to eat,' she said. 'Could we find a nicer bit of town, though?'

But Gracilis was shaking his head again. 'No, no, no. There's no time! I must continue my search!'

The Doctor was gentle but firm, almost as if he was a real doctor. 'Food and rest. You'll be no good to anyone till you've had those. And then – well, Rose and I are fond of a good search, aren't we, Rose?'

'Love 'em,' said Rose.

'So you tell us what you're looking for – and we'll look for it with you. Deal?'

'Er…' said Gracilis. But the Doctor had already grabbed his hand and shaken it. 'Deal.'

*

Once they got into the main part of the city the streets were much more crowded. 'It's like Oxford Street at Christmas!' gasped Rose, as the tenth or eleventh person shoved her out of the way.

'Rome's got a population of one million,' said the Doctor.

'Really?' said Rose.

'Yup.' He started counting off passers-by. 'One, two, three—'

'Yeah, all right, I believe you. But I think every single one of 'em's heading in the opposite direction to us!' She hopped out of the way of a particularly persistent pedestrian. 'And they're all drunk!'

'It's a festival day,' the Doctor explained.

'It is? Lucky us!'

The Doctor shook his head. 'It'd have been more surprising if it wasn't. To the Romans, almost every day is a festival of something or other.'

Rose grinned. 'Lucky them!'

Finally the Doctor managed to forge a path towards what Rose would call a small café, although it probably had some fancy Latin name. Most of its customers were buying food to take out, but there were a few tables for those who wanted to sit down – 'Sort of like Starbucks,' said Rose.

The Doctor fetched a pile of fruit pastries and three cups of spiced wine – which turned out to taste like boiled vinegar with cloves – while Rose led Gracilis to a bench.

Rose hadn't realised how pale the old man was until she saw the colour coming back to his face with the wine and the pastry. 'Thank you,' he said to them for about the thirtieth time. 'How can I ever repay you? You must let me give you a reward.' He began opening a pouch on his belt; there was the sound of coins chinking.

'Oh, we don't do rewards,' said the Doctor, putting up a hand to refuse.

'Really, we do this sort of thing for fun,' Rose told Gracilis, seeing his puzzled expression. 'So, what're you searching for, then?'

The old man's face blanched again and Rose felt quite alarmed. But he steadied himself and took a deep breath. 'My son,' he said. 'My handsome, clever son, Optatus. He has gone missing. A boy – I should say, a man – of just sixteen!'

'And you reckon he's in Rome somewhere, then?' asked Rose.

Gracilis sighed. 'I do not know. My family is currently residing in our country villa, but it has been searched, and the lands all around. I thought of Rome – you know what boys are, always far too keen for their own good on the wild ways of the city. But I have looked and I have asked and I have begged in a manner quite unfitting for my position, and not a trace have I found.'

The café's proprietor, a tubby man with food stains down his tunic, hadn't troubled to hide the fact that he was listening to their conversation with interest. 'Here, I know what you can do,' he suddenly interjected.

Gracilis jumped from his seat. 'You can help me find my son?'

'Well, no,' said the man. 'Not find him exactly.' Gracilis sank back down again. 'But I reckon I know who can.'

He came out from behind the counter and flopped down on the bench next to Rose. His fishy odour overcame even the vinegary wafts from the wine and she had to make an effort not to flinch.

'Well, don't keep us in suspense,' said the Doctor.

The man gave a loud sniff. 'There's this girl, see. They say she can tell the future, anything, just from looking at the stars.'

'An astrologer?' asked Gracilis.

'That's the very thing,' the chubby man replied. 'I heard she predicted that Hadrian was going to rebuild the Pantheon. And he is!'

'That's nothing,' put in a customer from the next bench, through a mouthful of bread and cheese. 'She told me that I was going to have a big row with my wife – and it came true!'

'Well, yeah,' said the chubby man, 'but you'd just been trying to chat up the girl in front of your wife. *I* could've predicted that. Anyway, I heard she's said the Empire's going to fall in a few centuries. I'm thinking of moving the family, just to be on the safe side.'

Rose tutted. 'Oh, come off it,' she said. 'Who are you trying to kid? Astrology's a load of rubbish.'

'You would say that,' said the Doctor. 'Typical Taurean.'

She raised her eyebrows at him. 'Come on. You're not telling me you believe in that stuff…'

But the Doctor shushed her as Gracilis pushed himself from his seat.

'Tell me, where is this famed woman? How can I find her?'

As the café owner gave directions, the Doctor and Rose got to their feet too, the Doctor cramming in the last of his pastry as he made ready to leave.

Gracilis turned to them. 'My friends, I am truly grateful for your assistance, and would be glad to offer you hospitality in my villa if ever you happen by, but I will trespass on your goodness no longer.'

'You must be joking,' said the Doctor. 'We're not going to miss an opportunity to meet a lady who can tell the future, are we, Rose?' And he looked at Rose and grinned.

She grinned back. 'Not a chance.'

TWO

The Doctor, Rose and Gracilis made their way to the Via Lata, passing by Trajan's Column itself, which pierced the sky with its carved tales of Trajan's victory over the Dacians. It looked even more impressive close up – marble panels spiralling away from a sort of temple thing at the bottom. ('That's got Trajan's ashes in it,' the Doctor said.) This nearby, Rose had to crane her neck right back to see the emperor's statue standing on the top, over 100 feet above her. There was a viewing platform at the top of the column and she could see the Doctor just itching to climb up to it, but Gracilis was a man on a mission and so they were forced to hurry on too.

Eventually they came to the place named by the café owner. An apartment in a block, it was not the most salubrious of locations, but it was a great deal better than the area in which they'd first arrived. Really, it wasn't all that different from the Powell Estate – several blocks of apartments were built around a courtyard, and there were even some shops on the ground floor, but selling olive oil and kitchenware rather than cigarettes and Chinese food.

They climbed up the stairs to the apartment in question,

where the Doctor took the lead and knocked on the door.

After a moment it opened slightly and a narrow-eyed man in a grubby tunic peered out at them. 'Well? What do you want?'

The Doctor smiled at him. 'We'd like to see the young lady who lives here. You know, the prophet? Astrologer?'

The man's demeanour changed instantly. Suddenly he was obsequious, gushing, as he pushed the door wide and stood back to let them in.

'Ah, my pleasure, gentlemen and lady, my very great pleasure. Allow me to introduce myself. My name is Balbus, and you shall see the lady, the reader of the stars, the interpreter of planets, she who knows what is to come. For only the smallest of small fees, you shall see her.'

'Cross her palm with silver,' muttered Rose. 'Nothing changes.'

She expected Gracilis to haggle at the sum mentioned, but he was obviously too anxious about his son to quibble over money, and he gave the man a handful of coins without protest.

The scruffy man led the way into a back room, where someone was sitting huddled in a corner.

'Visitors for you, Vanessa,' he said, rubbing his hands avariciously in the manner of someone who'd got a good bargain. 'Tell them what they want to know.'

The figure looked up, and Rose was taken aback. She'd unconsciously expected a fairground gypsy type, elderly and rosy-cheeked, a knowing smile on her face as she told of tall dark strangers and voyages across the sea. But this was just a girl – a thin, dark-skinned girl with haunted eyes.

'Yes, master.'

Rose turned to the Doctor, looking quizzical.

'She's a slave,' he mouthed back silently.

Gracilis sat down in front of the girl. 'You must tell me where to find my son!' he implored. 'I can give you his time and place of birth, all you need to know.'

The girl looked scared.

'Answer the gentleman, Vanessa,' said her owner, his grin like a wolf's.

In a soft voice, she began to ask Gracilis questions about Optatus, then reached out for a piece of parchment and began to work out calculations. They didn't mean much to Rose – she was never that keen on maths at the best of times, let alone trying to understand it upside-down – but she noticed that the Doctor's attention had been grabbed. He stared at the figures in a sort of frozen way for a few moments, before shaking his head as if to clear it and turning back to Gracilis.

Gracilis was looking eager, expectant. Rose felt sorry for him – not just because of his son, but because he was so desperate he'd been driven to ridiculous measures like this. The girl might seem nice enough, not the type to take advantage, but Rose couldn't say the same for her owner. Preying on the weak and wretched, that was obviously the game here – as if working out where a few stars were at the time of someone's birth could tell you where they'd gone off to sixteen years later.

Balbus's smile was getting more and more forced. 'Answer the gentleman,' he said again, after several more minutes had passed.

'Come on. Let us have our money's worth,' the Doctor told him. 'Can't calculate the movements of the heavens in two minutes, you know.'

The girl looked grateful and began scribbling down a few

more sums. Suddenly Rose realised something. The girl was playing for time! Of course she couldn't give Gracilis a true answer, so she was trying to think of what to say to him.

Perhaps the Doctor had realised that too. He sat down opposite the girl. 'Obviously I'm not dismissing your abilities, but I expect it's quite hard to work out something like this with so little information. You need to find out more about the boy, Optatus. And you need to see the place where he disappeared, I bet.'

She nodded desperately, her eyes seeming to plead with them. 'Yes, yes, I need to see the place where he disappeared.'

'Well, I'm sure your –' the Doctor paused, the word distasteful – '*owner* won't mind you popping along with us for a bit. Not in aid of such a good cause.'

But strangely her owner didn't seem that happy about the idea. 'I'm afraid I couldn't consider—' he began, but he got no further.

Gracilis thumped his fist on the table, causing the girl's pen to blot ink all over her calculations. 'Then let me buy her from you,' he said. 'Don't you understand, man, she's my only hope!'

'What, give up my little goldmine – I mean,' Balbus said, obsequious smile coming back into play, 'give up my sacred duty to protect my charge?'

'Oh, we can protect her, no problem,' said the Doctor breezily. 'I think this sounds like a jolly good idea all round. Gracilis here is a rich man. I'm sure you'll have no problem coming to some arrangement.'

Balbus shrugged. 'It is the Quinquatrus coming up. All those women, the tourists, they love to hear their futures. If I do not have Vanessa I will lose much money…'

Rose's toes curled in discomfort as she listened to them discussing a price for the girl – a human being was being bought and sold as if she was a table or a bag of apples or a jumble-sale coat.

Vanessa didn't seem that horrified, though; she seemed happy, eager, unable to believe her luck. Her life here couldn't be much fun and she obviously envisaged a better time serving Gracilis.

Finally, the negotiations complete, Gracilis, the Doctor and Rose left the apartment with Vanessa in tow.

'So, what now?' asked Rose.

'Just what I said,' replied the Doctor. 'I think it would help us all if we went back to Gracilis's villa and examined the spot where Optatus was last seen. If the invitation's still open, of course?'

He turned to the old man, who nodded eagerly. 'Yes, yes, if you think that's best.' He sighed. 'I could look in Rome for a year and never find him, even if he is here.'

'Yeah, it's not as if you've got photos of him you can hand out,' said Rose without thinking. The Doctor shot her a look. 'I mean – something to show people what he looks like,' she said hurriedly.

Gracilis smiled sadly. 'Ah, if you wish to see what my beloved child looks like – well, just wait till we arrive at the villa.'

Gracilis's carriage was waiting outside the city gates and they all climbed in. The Doctor indicated by gesture that he wanted Rose to stick closely to Vanessa, but she would have done anyway. The girl had hardly said a word since they'd left the apartment, but Rose was determined to engage her in conversation.

'So, d'you come from Rome?' she tried, as a nice easy

question to start with. But it seemed to alarm Vanessa, who stayed silent. She had another go. 'How old are you?'

This time the girl answered. 'Sixteen,' she whispered.

'And how long have you been doing this astrology lark?'

Again Vanessa didn't answer, but Rose was shocked to see tears beginning to trickle down her cheeks. She impulsively grabbed the girl in a hug. 'Hey, don't cry! I'm sorry, I won't ask you anything else, not if you don't want to tell me.' But now the girl had started crying, it seemed she couldn't stop. Rose held her as the sobs heaved through her body, rocking her gently, comforting. Wondering just what had happened to this girl to make her so very scared.

The journey was slow and Rose thought longingly of trains and cars. Still, she supposed a horse-drawn (well, actually donkey-drawn) carriage was a lot more environmentally friendly, even if it was a long and bumpy ride. She'd been surprised to learn they wouldn't get to the villa that day and would have to stay the night at a guesthouse along the way. She hoped it would at least give her a chance to speak to Vanessa with no one else looking on, but slaves went in a different part of the building. Rose wondered what the slave quarters must be like, considering how grotty the bed she was given was – she spent the night half sleeping, half lying awake having worrying thoughts about Roman hygiene and potential infestation, trying to tell herself that any itching was entirely in her imagination...

They left the next morning when the sun was barely up. It would probably take them the whole day to get to the villa, so Gracilis wanted to make an early start. Rose was happy, though, if it meant they wouldn't be spending another night at a way station.

The old man showed no interest in breakfasting, but as the sun started to climb in the sky the Doctor jumped off the vehicle and picked them all early figs from a tree growing wild by the roadside. 'Worked out the date. It's AD 120,' he whispered to Rose as he handed her some fruit. 'Hadrian's the emperor. Don't worry. I'm picking up all the goss.'

Gracilis was obviously eager to get back and let Vanessa start to track Optatus. Rose felt the girl shiver at that – she was as convinced as she could be that Vanessa had no gifts, no mystical powers, and she wondered what the charming old Roman would do if he discovered he'd spent all that money on a slave for nothing. For now, though, he seemed sweet-tempered, if worried, sitting over the other side of the carriage talking quietly to the Doctor. Still, Rose began to plan rescue strategies in her head. Just in case.

Despite Gracilis's expectations, Vanessa seemed more cheerful after a night's rest and even responded hesitantly to some of Rose's remarks about the scenery. Encouraged, Rose pressed on. 'I'm from Britain – Britannia?' she said. 'You know, where this Emperor Hadrian bloke built his wall, yeah?'

'Oh, Hadrian's Wall. Meant to keep out the barbarians,' said Vanessa.

'What, like Celtic football fans?' said Rose, laughing.

Vanessa looked puzzled, but laughed too. For a moment, Rose thought she was going to say more, reveal something about herself – but she didn't.

It was dusk by the time they reached the villa, but there was just enough light left for Rose to see what it was like. She had been expecting something resembling a stately home, but it was more like a farm, even if an incredibly posh one. There were a number of buildings covered with rather ugly stucco decoration surrounding a courtyard with fountains and fish ponds. There were elaborate mosaics and elegant statues. There were fields of crops, an orchard of peaches and almonds bursting with blossom, stables for donkeys and yards for chickens and geese.

'Not a bad place, this,' murmured the Doctor, as they went inside.

A short, dumpy woman came running to meet them. She looked as if her natural state was kindness and jollity, but at the moment her face was drawn and anxious. 'Did you find him?' she cried, ignoring everyone but Gracilis.

Gracilis shook his head sadly, then introduced the woman as his wife, Marcia, mother of Optatus. 'But these good people are here to help!' he told her. 'This slave –' he indicated Vanessa – 'is a prophet of great power. Once she has discovered more of Optatus, she will find him for us.' He paused for a second. 'Is there word from Ursus?'

'He assures me it will still be ready for tomorrow, as promised,' Marcia answered.

Marcia offered them food, but they had eaten on the way. The light was now fading rapidly and the few oil lamps did not really offer sufficient illumination – it would seem it was the habit to retire early and rise with the sun.

'Tomorrow I will show you my son,' Gracilis promised as he summoned slaves to show the Doctor and Rose to guest rooms. 'I am sure you will prove to be the answer to my prayers.'

But Rose, as she tossed and turned in the unfamiliar – yet thankfully clean – bed, wasn't sure of that at all.

*

The Doctor was already out and about when Rose made her sleepy way downstairs the next morning. She finally found him in an orchard, sitting beneath a tree as peach blossoms sprinkled his hair like a snow shower.

'Way to go for the detective work,' she said.

'Hercule Poirot could solve any case by just sitting back and thinking,' he told her.

'You with a twirly moustache!' She laughed. 'Go with the sideburns, that would.'

'I expect it would make me look even more sophisticated,' he said haughtily.

Rose grinned. 'Go on, then. Grow a twirly moustache. I dare you.'

'Fine!' he said, gesturing at his upper lip. 'I'm growing one now. Look!'

She peered closely, pretending to believe him, but collapsed in a gale of laughter after a moment, and the Doctor joined her. 'Maybe not,' he said.

'So, what's the plan?' Rose asked after they'd both calmed down.

'Gracilis is preparing something,' the Doctor told her. 'We're to meet him in half an hour.'

They talked of nothing in particular until a slave came to fetch them. He led them to a grove near the villa's main entrance. Proud peacocks strode across the grass and through the neat, ordered flower beds, and water trickled from the mouths of stone nymphs and fauns into a little pond. The only discordant note was struck by a human being; a tall, thick-set, scowling man, alien in this environment of richness and beauty. He was slumped against the base of a statue – at least Rose assumed it was a statue; it had a sheet draped over it.

Gracilis, Marcia and Vanessa were approaching the grove from a different direction and the unpleasant-looking man struggled to his feet as he saw them arrive.

'Ah, Ursus, my dear fellow,' said Gracilis. 'I trust all is prepared for the unveiling?'

The man nodded curtly.

'Excellent!' Gracilis turned to the Doctor and Rose. Rose noticed that Vanessa pretty much didn't exist in his eyes, unless he was actually talking about or to her. 'This is Aulus Valerius Ursus. He's a local lad but is fast becoming the talk of the Empire! I think I may say with little fear of contradiction that he is one of the greatest sculptors of our day. He rarely undertakes commissions for private citizens, so I was greatly honoured when he agreed to create a work for me to celebrate my beloved son.'

'The money you offered, I could hardly refuse,' said the man, with a rapacious smile that reminded Rose of Vanessa's former owner, Balbus.

Gracilis gave a sad chuckle. 'It is true that the advantage of being a very rich man is that things can sometimes be bought which are not normally for sale. And yet I cannot buy the one thing I desire above all others: the return of my son.'

He stepped forward and took hold of the cloth covering the statue. 'Still, it is my hope that this will bring us closer to that happy event.'

With a sharp flick of his wrist, the sheet fell away and the statue was revealed. It was of a young boy striking a noble pose. The statue was of gleaming white marble, but its lips, eyes and hair had been painted in bright colours – Rose considered that a bit tasteless personally, only one step away from drawing on a moustache and glasses in felt-tip.

Gracilis sighed heavily. 'This day was supposed to be a celebration,' he said, turning to the Doctor and Rose. 'The Liberalia, the day on which my son took at last the *toga virilis* and became a man in the eyes of the world.' He gestured at the stone boy. 'This was to commemorate that momentous day. But at least it may aid us in our plight.'

'This is Optatus,' said Marcia, dissolving into tears and flinging herself at the statue, hugging its knees tightly as though to stop her son leaving again. 'And now you will be able to find him.'

THREE

Gracilis led his weeping wife back towards the main house. Vanessa was told to follow them; Marcia would tell her more about Optatus's birth. Ursus seemed about to go too, but the Doctor stopped him with a gesture.

'Pretty impressive stuff,' he said, indicating the sculpture.

'All my "stuff" is impressive,' Ursus replied.

'Ah, I see. Do I see? Yes, I think I do,' said the Doctor, nodding. He half turned away, letting the man go, but then suddenly pounced with another question. 'You must have seen a lot of Optatus, working on this. What do you think has happened to him?'

Ursus shrugged. 'How should I know? Sons of rich men, they get kidnapped. It happens.'

'Pretty rubbish kidnappers,' put in Rose. 'They've had him for days and not even bothered to ask for a ransom.'

'Then he has gone off on his own somewhere. Perhaps he has been attacked by highwaymen, perhaps he is drunk in a tavern somewhere. It is none of my concern.'

The Doctor seemed to consider this. 'Yes, could be... Of course, we're miles from the city and he took no transport... Still, you could be right.'

Rose could tell he didn't believe it in the slightest. Or perhaps he just didn't want to believe it, didn't want a mundane solution. Perhaps, for the Doctor, any little mystery to investigate was better than none at all.

'When did you last see the boy?' asked the Doctor, in his best detective voice.

Ursus seemed reluctant to answer. 'Four days ago,' he muttered eventually. 'My work was almost complete, but he visited me in my studio to observe the finishing touches. I have a studio set up near the stables in order to work here.'

'Must be interesting,' said the Doctor. 'I'd like to come and visit you there.'

Ursus shook his head firmly. 'I allow no one to see me at work. No one.'

'Ah,' said the Doctor. Then he began counting on his fingers. 'Hang on, four days ago? That's the very day young Master Optatus disappeared. Blimey, you could even have been the last person to see him!'

'Perhaps.' The sculptor shrugged. 'How do I know?'

'Well, I think we really will have to visit that excellent studio of yours, then. Start of the trail and all that.'

Ursus bristled. 'I have told you, no one is allowed inside my studio. I am an artist and I do not permit it!'

'Not your studio, though, is it?' said Rose. 'This place belongs to Gracilis, and I bet he'd let us in there. Seeing as we're after his son and all.'

Ursus stepped forward and for a moment Rose thought he was going to hit her. She tensed. But instead he reached out a hand and lightly touched her cheek. His hands were enormous, thick sausage fingers encased in stiff leather gloves, not the sort of hands she associated with artists. But his clumsy physical appearance obviously belied his skill, as proved by the superbly lifelike sculpture of Optatus.

'*You* can come to my studio,' the sculptor said to Rose, and she suddenly realised the inevitability of what was to come next. 'I have a commission, a statue of a goddess. You are young and beautiful. You will be her. That is the only way you will get to see my studio – if I make you a goddess.'

This is what it had all been leading up to. Arriving in Rome, rescuing Gracilis, being invited to his villa, meeting Ursus – it had always been going to happen, because it was all there to bring them to this moment, to the creation of a statue that would travel across hundreds of years and half of Europe to end up in a basement room in the British Museum in the twenty-first century.

'All right,' said Rose.

The Doctor had sat down on the edge of the pond and was dangling his feet in the water, smiling at the small shiny fish that swam up to nibble his toes. Rose slipped off her sandals and joined him.

'So, you're gonna be a model, then,' he said. 'Rose the model. Model Rose.'

She nodded glumly. 'Yeah, looks like it. You know, I thought it'd be a bit more glam than this – posing for a caveman in a toga in someone's stables.'

'It may not be glamorous, but it is important. We need to have a look in that studio.'

'You think Ursus is dodgy?' Rose asked.

The Doctor just shrugged. 'Don't know. Could be. I mean, I didn't *like* him – but that doesn't mean he's dodgy. Although it hints at it, seeing as I'm such a good judge of character. Anyway, best not to neglect any possibilities.'

Rose sighed. 'I wonder how Vanessa's getting on with

Mrs Gracilis. Poor kid. I reckon that Balbus bloke put her up to this astrology lark and now she's stuck with it.'

'You think she can't really tell the future?' asked the Doctor.

Rose laughed incredulously. 'Course she can't! No one can. I mean, I know there are some people who see stuff – but that's, like, aliens and rifts and that. Come on, you could tell she's a fake!'

The Doctor raised an eyebrow. 'Remember what they said about her in the café. The things she predicted.'

'You've been watching too much Living TV on the scanner, you have,' Rose said, scarcely believing she had to explain this to the Doctor, of all people. 'She could've guessed about the building thing, or heard rumours. And just 'cause we know the Roman Empire really is gonna fall doesn't mean anyone who talked about it's a prophet. They're probably just, you know, pessimistic.'

'Good logic,' said the Doctor.

'Thank you,' said Rose. She thought for a minute. 'Mind you, there is something a bit weird about her. I wish she'd told me a bit more about herself. Wouldn't even tell me where she came from. This TARDIS thing that's in my head – OK, so I can understand languages, which is, you know, all right, but it don't half make it tricky to work out accents. I guess she must be speaking Latin, 'cause everyone else can understand her, but I don't think she's from Rome, though… She knows about Hadrian's Wall, but I don't think she's British… I'll keep trying, but—'

The Doctor was suddenly as still as the stone faun by his side. 'So,' he said after a moment, 'you don't believe this girl can tell the future.'

'No, I don't,' said Rose.

'So, would you like to explain to me exactly how this Latin-speaking sixteen-year-old is aware of a wall that Hadrian won't even start to think about building until at least next year? That's what I call a really good guess.'

Rose just gaped at him.

The Doctor had gone off to talk to people around the estate, to try to work out when and where Optatus was last seen. He'd asked Rose to find Vanessa and see again if she could get her talking. 'But don't let her suspect you know her secret,' he said. 'Not for now, anyway.'

'So, are we thinking she's dangerous?' Rose asked. 'Because she doesn't seem dangerous. I liked her. Did you like her?'

'I didn't not like her,' said the Doctor.

'There you go, then. Judge of character and all that. If there's a bad guy here, it's that Ursus, I'm sure of it.'

'Just be careful,' the Doctor told her.

She'd found Vanessa in the main house with Marcia. Marcia had a piece of needlework on her knee, but was ignoring it in favour of telling Vanessa the entire life history of Optatus.

'And then in his fifth summer he fell from a peach tree and hurt his arm…' She paused expectantly.

Vanessa said, 'Ah, the, er, typical adventurousness of the Capricorn, coming under the… hostile influence of… Jupiter.'

'Of course, of course,' Marcia agreed. 'Come on in, my dear, and sit down,' she said to Rose. She waved a hand at a slave, who went off and returned seconds later with a cup of wine for Rose. 'My dear, I have to tell you how much I love your hair,' she continued. 'Blonde is so fashionable!'

'Er, thanks,' said Rose. 'Well, you know what they say, blondes have more fun…'

'Was it a slave's?'

'No,' said Rose, confused, 'it's mine.'

'Oh, you've had it dyed,' said Marcia, nodding knowledgeably. 'Well, it really suits you.'

Rose decided it would be sensible to leave the topic of ancient hairdressing before she tripped herself up. She turned to Vanessa. 'So, picked up any clues yet?'

The young girl gave a nervous smile. 'I feel that Optatus is favoured by the gods,' she said. 'The stars at his birth were… auspicious. I am sure that he is safe.'

'Great,' said Rose, sitting down.

'Yes, my mind is greatly relieved!' said Marcia, smiling.

'Well, while Vanessa's, er, considering his astrological destiny, we're trying to figure out who saw him last. Tell me, Marcia, what do you know about this Ursus bloke?'

Marcia's eyes widened. 'You think Ursus may be connected with my son's disappearance? I shall have my husband evict him from the estate at once!'

Rose hastened to calm her down. 'No, look, I'm just asking. Gracilis said he was a local boy, right? So you must know him. And even if he is connected – I'm not saying he is,' she added quickly, as Marcia's mouth flew open, 'we don't want him getting the wind up or anything. Keep them where you can see them, that's the thing.'

Marcia nodded reluctantly. She thought for a moment and then said, 'I don't really know much about him. He was rather a clumsy, unpleasant child, as I recall. I remember being surprised to hear he was planning to take up art.'

It was the sort of story that never changed, Rose thought. An unpopular child, teased and ridiculed but determined to fulfil his ambitions and prove his tormentors wrong. But the ending happened less frequently: boy makes good against all the odds. Because, as she'd seen for herself, that's what had happened. After years of humiliation, the boy – now a man – had suddenly found the success he had been seeking, perhaps more than he'd ever dreamed of.

'It was – oh, I'm not sure how long ago,' Marcia told her. 'Suddenly we began to hear his name everywhere. His statues appeared in the temples and shrines of Rome itself, and they were so admired. We thought they must be by some other artist of the same name, but no, it was the Ursus we knew. My husband pursued him for some time before he would agree to take on our commission.' She sighed. 'And how thankful I am. It comforts me to know I can still gaze on the face of my child, even in this time of darkness.'

Rose didn't say anything, didn't suggest to Marcia that if they hadn't persuaded Ursus to produce his sculpture of Optatus, the whole 'time of darkness' thing might have been avoided altogether.

Suddenly Marcia thumped a fist on her knee. 'Of course!' she said. 'We first saw a statue by Ursus when we were in Rome – I remember now. It was the festival of Fortuna. That means it is almost ten months ago.'

Vanessa started.

'You all right?' Rose said.

The girl nodded, but was staring into the distance. 'Almost ten months,' she said under her breath.

'We believed Fortuna had smiled on us when he agreed to craft our son,' said Marcia sadly. 'Now I believe we may have offended her.'

The name 'Fortuna' reverberated around Rose's head.

That was what it said under her statue in the British Museum. And perhaps, soon, she would discover exactly how the statue got there.

'Ursus wants to do a sculpture of me,' she told them.

Marcia looked surprised for a second, though she quickly hid it. 'But that is charming!' she said. 'I know my husband has given him permission to work in the studio here for as long as he wishes.' She smiled indulgently. 'I believe he fancies himself a patron of the arts. Anyway, you must stay as our guest until the work is complete.'

'I don't want to put you out…' said Rose, but Marcia was already doing the good hostess bit and shushing her protests.

'It will be a delight to have a young person around while my son –' her poised manner faltered for a moment – 'while my son is missing. I shall appreciate the company.'

'We're gonna get him back,' said Rose awkwardly. 'The Doctor and me – and Vanessa,' she added hurriedly. 'You know, with her predictions and that.'

The young girl flushed.

Rose remembered what the Doctor had said about getting her talking, but it was awkward with Marcia there. So she said, 'Actually, I think we could do with her help right now. While the Doctor's tracing Optatus's movements, Vanessa could be… picking up vibes, that sort of thing.'

Marcia nodded knowledgeably. 'Yes of course.' She waved a hand to dismiss Vanessa, and the girl followed Rose out of the room.

They wandered into the courtyard. Slaves passed them, carrying baskets of fruit or freshly baked bread.

'Ooh, love that smell,' said Rose, as a tray of loaves wafted past.

'I... I believe Optatus walked through this courtyard,' said Vanessa nervously.

Rose gave a laugh. 'You don't say! Look, it's all right. I'm not after any hocus-pocus stuff. I just thought you could do with a break. Come on.' She led Vanessa back to the grove where Optatus's statue stood and they sat down together on the grass.

'He looks so young,' Rose murmured, gazing at the statue. 'Sweet sixteen. Same age as you.'

Vanessa nodded. 'I think so.'

Rose darted a look at her. 'You're not sure?'

'It's... hard to keep track sometimes.'

'So, what star sign are you?'

'Scorpio,' said Vanessa. 'Determined and forceful.'

Rose laughed. 'Well, now I'm convinced! You don't believe in that stuff, do you.'

It was a statement, not a question.

The girl looked scared, so Rose hurried to reassure her. 'It's all right. I know it's a load of rubbish, but I bet you were forced into it somehow. Am I right?'

Hesitantly, Vanessa nodded.

'So, here's what's gonna happen. The Doctor and I will find Optatus. That's what we do, sort things out. You can stick with us. We'll tell everyone we need you. Hopefully no one'll ask you about aspects or Saturn or anything, but you obviously know how to talk the talk if you have to. Then, when it's all sorted, we'll get you home somehow. Get you out of all this.'

Rose thought of her own life at sixteen. GCSEs, falling in love, dropping out of school, leaving home. All ended up in disaster and heartbreak, of course, and she'd never want to go back – but whatever else it was, it was living. What

Vanessa had been going through – well, she didn't know the details, but she'd be prepared to bet it didn't really come under that category.

Rose had thought Vanessa would be pleased. But when she looked at the girl, she saw that she had begun to cry.

'Hey, what is it?' she said, folding her into a hug.

'I don't have a home,' said the girl. 'Not any more.'

FOUR

Vanessa was still crying softly when the Doctor bounded into the grove. It didn't seem to bother him, though. He plonked himself down on the grass beside them.

'OK, here's what we've got. Optatus visits Ursus in his workshop every day for a couple of weeks. The general impression the boy gave was that the sculpture was still at the planning stages, but as no one was allowed in to see what was going on we've got no evidence to back that up. Then a few days ago, he gets up early, breakfasts on a couple of wheat biscuits, yum yum, and heads off to the studio. And that's it. No one sees him leave – which isn't necessarily suspicious, but what is odd is that Ursus suddenly declares the statue is almost finished, needing only a few more days of finishing touches.'

'Is that quick, then?' asked Rose, whose experience in these fields extended not much further than a clay pot in Year Eight art lessons.

'I'd say so,' said the Doctor. 'You wouldn't need a model the whole time, but for the statue itself I would have thought months, years even. I'm not a master sculptor, of course…'

Rose grinned. 'What, you mean you never had lessons with Michelangelo or anything?'

The Doctor gave her a warning look and Rose realised she'd slipped up. 'Sorry,' she whispered.

'That's all right,' he whispered back, then looked thoughtful. 'Perhaps I should pop back to the Renaissance some time. *The Doctor's "David"* has quite a ring to it.' He raised his voice again. 'Other thing is, if the statue was that near completion, Ursus must've been working on the thing itself, rather than preliminaries. And marble might be all white and shiny but it's not clean to work with. Dirt, dust, you name it. Yet no one ever noticed Ursus or Optatus in desperate need of a wash.'

'So… he wasn't doing a sculpture after all?' said Rose.

But the Doctor pointed up at the statue. 'Now there we do have evidence,' he said. 'Anyway, it's imperative that we get inside his studio. Find out his working practices.'

'Well, I'm all ready to be model girl,' said Rose.

The Doctor nodded. 'Good. Tell you what, though. Let's go and have a look now, shall we?'

Rose grinned. 'You can't sit still for two minutes, you can't!' She turned to Vanessa, who had stopped crying but still didn't appear to be a barrel of laughs.

'Look, d'you wanna stay here? If anyone comes, just say you're meditating on the statue or something. Tell them we told you to.'

Vanessa nodded gratefully, so the Doctor and Rose walked off alone.

'What's the matter with her?' the Doctor asked. 'Is something bad going to happen next Wednesday?'

Rose frowned at him. 'She can't really see into the future, she said so. I told her we'd get her home and she said she didn't have one. And got upset about it.'

'Maybe her home's just a very long way away,' said the Doctor.

'And in the meantime she's stuck here as a slave.'

He nodded. 'I don't like it any more than you do. But some slaves do lead happy lives, you know. Or they're given their freedom, or buy it.'

'Doesn't make it right,' Rose muttered.

'No,' he said. 'It doesn't.' Suddenly he grabbed Rose's arm and pulled her behind a tree.

'What?' she mouthed.

He waited a few moments and then let her go. 'Ursus,' he said. 'Just saw him.'

'Which means he's not in his workshop!' Rose realised.

'So what better time could there be for us to visit?'

They hurried off towards the stables, keeping an eye out for any sign of a returning Ursus. The Doctor tried the door of the workshop, but it was locked.

'Sonic screwdriver?' said Rose, looking at the Doctor's belt.

'Back in the villa,' the Doctor replied. 'Do you know how frustrating it is not to have pockets? I feel like I've lost a part of me. I keep going to stick my hands in them and they're not there.'

'You need one of those little pouches to hang on your belt,' Rose told him. She reached up to her head. A ringlet fell over her shoulder as she detached a silver hairpin and handed it to him. 'Back to the old-fashioned methods, I guess.'

He nodded. 'When in Rome…'

Rose kept a lookout, but it didn't take the Doctor long to pick the lock and Ursus didn't appear. Finally, the door swung open. The Doctor strode in like he owned the place.

The first room was more or less empty, containing just a small table holding a jug, a cup and a hunk of bread. But as they went through it and entered the next one, they saw a very attractive young man sitting on a bench. He jumped up as they entered and bowed his head.

'Ooh, hello,' said Rose.

'Hello!' the Doctor echoed. 'I'm the Doctor and this is Rose. Who are you?'

The boy looked ner vous. 'My name is Tiro. Forgive me, but do you have the permission of my master, Ursus, to be here? He allows no one in his workshop.'

'Oh, he doesn't mind us. He told us to pop in. Told us he'd left the door unlocked specially. I mean, he doesn't usually leave the door unlocked, does he?'

Tiro shook his head.

'There you go, then.'

Rose grinned. 'We wanted to check it all out, you see? I'm gonna be posing for him.' She did a pirouette. 'Next top model, that's me.' She looked at Tiro, taking in his slim, muscled figure, his perfect features and his softly waved hair. 'Just a guess, but you're here to pose too, right?'

Tiro nodded. 'My master bought me for that purpose, yes.'

Rose pulled a face. 'You know, I don't think I'm ever gonna get used to that.' She shook her head at Tiro's inquiring look. 'Doesn't matter. So, how d'you like being a model, then?'

He smiled at her. 'I don't know. I haven't started yet. I'm a bit nervous.'

'I know what you mean,' Rose agreed.

'Fighting monsters, exploring moons, defeating evil –

nothing compared with standing still for a few hours while some bloke chips away with a chisel,' put in the Doctor.

Rose told Tiro to ignore him.

She moved over to look at a pile of odds and ends in the corner – a spear, a bow, a horn, a hat with little wings attached. 'Everything a god or goddess might need,' she said. She picked up the horn and struck a pose. 'What d'ya think?'

'I'm sure you'll bring me luck,' said the Doctor. He walked past her, and began opening doors and peering through. 'That's odd,' he commented.

'What's odd?' said Rose, rolling her eyes. The Doctor found oddness everywhere.

He frowned. 'Well, presumably Ursus is about to start two new statues – one of you, one of Tiro here. But there's not a scrap of stone in the place.'

Rose shrugged. 'Maybe he hasn't got it yet. Rome probably doesn't do next-day delivery.'

The Doctor's ears had pricked up. 'Aha, that sounds like the ursine footsteps of the man himself. I'll ask him.'

The door opened and Ursus entered. His face became thunderous at the sight of the Doctor and Rose. 'I thought I informed you that no one is allowed in my workshop,' he bellowed, and turned to glower at Tiro, who shrank back nervously.

The Doctor stepped forward. 'Don't blame the boy,' he said. 'And don't blame us either. You sadly neglected to tell Rose what time you required her for her sitting, so, being pleasant, neighbourly folks, we merely popped in to find out when would be convenient for you. That's all.'

Ursus seemed to calm down slightly – although not enough for Rose's liking. She had the distinct impression that he was a dangerous man to cross.

'Be here at the third hour after sunrise,' he grunted at her, and she had to fight back the urge to salute sarcastically.

'All right if the Doctor comes along and watches?' she asked, knowing the answer.

'No!' the sculptor exploded. 'No, it is not all right! No one is permitted to see me working!'

'I only asked,' said Rose.

'I noticed you don't seem to have any stone ready for your sculptures,' the Doctor said, wilfully ignoring Ursus's blatant desire for them to leave instantly. 'I happen to know a few merchants, best marble in the business, I—'

'It's on its way,' Ursus barked, before the Doctor could develop his lie any further.

'Fine, fine. No need to thank me for my very kind offer,' said the Doctor.

'Your offer? Pa! You know marble merchants, you say. You break into my studio. You are a rival, come to steal my ideas!'

'No, I'm not,' said the Doctor indignantly.

'He's no master sculptor,' put in Rose. 'He said so himself only half an hour ago.'

'Right,' said the Doctor. 'Glad that's sorted.' He turned away and began to examine a table full of sculpting tools.

'You are trying my patience,' said the sculptor.

'Oh, I'm sorry,' said the Doctor, still bending over the table and making not the slightest effort to stop what he was doing. He held up a chisel. 'You know, you really do keep your instruments in perfect condition. You wouldn't know that any of these had ever been used.'

'I am a careful workman,' said Ursus.

'I'll say you are,' said the Doctor, sounding impressed.

'Even your workshop is spotless. Not a trace of marble dust anywhere. Still, I suppose there are slaves to clear up after you.'

'No one is allowed in my workshop,' Ursus reiterated. 'No one except my subjects. Gracilis does not come in here. His wife does not come in here. Even slaves do not come in here. All respect my need for privacy to create art. The only person who does not is you.'

The Doctor looked astounded. 'What gave you that idea? We're leaving this minute, aren't we, Rose?'

'Right now,' she agreed, sketching a little half-wave of farewell to Tiro, who grinned at her.

'Talking of being a careful workman,' said the Doctor, as they sauntered slowly over towards the door, 'I suppose that's why you wear those gloves, to protect your hands. Bit of a trendsetter there. I don't think I've seen anyone else—'

But they were through the doorway by then and the door was slammed shut on them. A key turned loudly in the lock.

'Obviously doesn't want to share his fashion tips,' said the Doctor. He looked up at the sun, measuring its position in the sky with what Rose assumed was an expert eye. 'Come on. I reckon it's nearly time for dinner.'

Rose wanted a word with Marcia before dinner, but that didn't take long. Grinning at her achievement, she hurried back to her room to get ready. She was slightly nervous about dinner, but after living with her mum for most of her life she reckoned she could cope with virtually anything in the food line.

When she finally went in to dinner, it wasn't just food she had to cope with, though. First a slave washed her feet, which was weird – no one had washed her feet for her since her mum had rinsed off Tenby sand with a bucket of seawater while she sat on a deckchair eating ice cream. Then she was led to what was pretty much a bed, and she worked out she was supposed to lie down on her front, as that was what Marcia and Gracilis were doing. The Doctor, however, propped himself up on his side, resting on one elbow, and Rose thought that looked a much easier position to eat from so she copied him instead.

She had this idea that Roman meals were all dormice and flamingos, more pet shop than pizzeria. But this wasn't at all like that. Rose was served some unidentified meat smothered in a strong-smelling sauce, with ordinary, recognisable vegetables like beans and asparagus on the side. She looked around her for some cutlery – but there was none to be seen.

The Doctor guessed what she was doing and grinned. 'They haven't invented forks yet and no one bothers with a knife,' he told her, picking up a piece of food with his fingers and popping it in his mouth.

She grimaced. 'Gross! It's all covered in sauce.'

'*Garum*,' said the Doctor. 'Ferment fish guts for a couple of months and you've got something strong enough to disguise the taste of rotten meat. No freezers, you see.'

Rose thought she might be sick. 'I might just stick to the veg,' she said. 'When do they invent pizza?'

'If you want a Four Seasons or a Vegetarian Hot, you'll be waiting a few centuries,' the Doctor told her.

'How about I order now, give them plenty of time.'

The Doctor grinned. 'Oh, and it's considered polite to belch after the meal,' he added.

'Then they're gonna have to think I'm rude,' Rose

announced firmly.

After they'd finished, a slave came round to wash their hands, while another slave brought in fruit and nuts and little honeyed cakes, which were rather more to Rose's taste.

Vanessa was nowhere to be seen during the meal – Rose wondered if she was still outside, sitting in the dusk by Optatus's statue, or if she was somewhere in the house with the other slaves. She thought she'd better check on the girl after dinner. Leaving the Doctor in conversation with Marcia and Gracilis, hearing all sorts of boring gossip about all sorts of boring people that they expected the Doctor to know, she slipped out of the house and down to the grove. Sure enough, Vanessa was still there.

Rose sat down beside her in the gloom and produced a hunk of bread that she'd managed to smuggle out. 'Here,' she said. 'I was worried you'd not had anything to eat. Sorry it's not much.'

Vanessa smiled her thanks. 'You're very kind.'

Rose shrugged. 'My pleasure. Look, why don't you come inside?'

'I don't know what to do,' said Vanessa hopelessly. 'I've never been in a house like this before. I don't know how I'm supposed to behave. They flog slaves who don't do the right thing, I'm sure.'

'But you're here as an astrologer, not a normal slave,' said Rose, trying to reassure her. 'They won't flog you, I won't let 'em. Look, how about this? We tell them that you need to commune with the stars in meditation, or something, that it's an essential part of your astrologer's rituals. They'll let you do anything then. They think you're going to get their son back. No flogging.'

'Except when they don't get their son back and realise I've been deceiving them.'

Rose gave her a mock-offended look. 'Hey! I told you, me and the Doctor were on the case. We're gonna get him back!' She sighed. 'But first, I've gotta pose for this statue. I'm expected to get there at three hours after sunrise. When on earth's that? Am I supposed to sit up watching for the sun to appear and then go "one hippopotamus, two hippopotamus" for three hours?'

Vanessa smiled finally. 'I'll wake you,' she said. 'I don't sleep much – not any more.'

'It's a deal,' said Rose. 'Look, there's something I want to get done before the light goes completely, so I'd better head back now.'

But she didn't move. The sun was going down and she couldn't seem to tear her eyes away from it.

All these dramas going on around her. Gracilis and Marcia, desperate for the return of their son. Ursus, with his lust for artistic fame. Vanessa's worries and fears. The slaves – who knew what they were hoping, dreaming? And yet in 2,000 years' time, they'd all be forgotten. Things that were life and death today would mean nothing even to the next generation, let alone those living in the twenty-first century. By the time she was born, the people here would be dust, the villa rubble. The only thing that would survive was a statue of a goddess, and who knew what it would endure over that time?

To the setting sun, the time between where Rose was now and where she had come from was no more than a blink. But to Rose – who'd been to the dawn of humanity and the very end of the Earth – it suddenly seemed an eternity.

Vanessa finished the piece of bread.

'Come on, then,' Rose said, and got up.

They walked together back to the house, and didn't look back.

FIVE

Rose was ripped from a dream about talking cats the next morning by Vanessa shaking her shoulder. 'Time to get up,' the girl said, as Rose yawned and tried to remember where she was. It took her a few minutes to force herself out of bed, yawning the whole time.

'Do you think Ursus will be able to capture the bags under my eyes OK?' she said as she stared at herself in the circle of polished bronze that served as a mirror. 'What time is it?'

'Two hours after sunrise,' Vanessa told her. 'You've got an hour before you have to be at the studio.'

'You'd think it'd be more in Ursus's interests to let me have my beauty sleep,' grumbled Rose, but she started to get ready anyway.

Vanessa helped her to do her hair, which took up most of the time they had at their disposal. Finally Rose was ready to go.

'Look, why don't you come with me?' she suggested to Vanessa. 'I'm not saying it'll be much fun, but I wouldn't mind the company. Keep you out of the way of everyone else too. I mean, Ursus has got a slave in there – he can't really object to me bringing one, whatever he says. Anyway, the way they treat slaves like furniture round here, he'll probably not even notice you.'

Vanessa smiled. 'Yes, I'd like to come.'

They crossed the courtyard, heading to the workshop by the stables. The Doctor was already up and about, and they waved to him in passing.

The studio door was locked, so Rose banged a fist on it. 'Remember, eyes and ears open,' she whispered to Vanessa while they were waiting. 'You know, in case he's a baddie.'

Vanessa might have replied, but just then the studio door was flung open by Ursus. He scowled as he saw her – probably not the sort of greeting someone like Kate Moss would get, but she could take it. She stepped inside, Vanessa close behind.

'Get her out of here,' Ursus growled, nodding his head towards the slave girl. 'I keep telling you and your doctor friend, I don't allow an audience while I'm working – even slaves.'

Rose put on an imperious air. 'So who's gonna look after me, then? What if I need someone to fix my hair, or get me a drink or something?'

Ursus stumped over to a table and picked up a jug. He slopped some wine into a goblet and held it out to Rose. 'There. There's your drink. Your hair's fine. Now *get out*!'

This last was to Vanessa, who fairly fled out of the door. Rose was half tempted to follow her. But this was all part of her destiny, wasn't it? She had to pose for the statue. And the Doctor was relying on her to investigate Ursus too, in case he knew anything about Optatus's disappearance. She gulped down the bitter wine – she still couldn't bear the taste, but it might help her to relax a bit.

Ursus walked through to the next room and Rose followed. There was no Tiro there today, which gave Rose a slight pang of disappointment.

'So, how d'you want me?' she asked, but Ursus ignored her. He moved over to a table and started sorting through his tools.

Rose sat down on a bench, awaiting instructions. She looked around the room – there was one thing different from how it had been the day before: a tall, covered shape in the corner. A work in progress? She hoped Ursus wasn't spreading himself too thin, because she wanted to get this over with and she really, really hoped it wouldn't take too long. She had a horrible feeling, though, that it would. Days, maybe weeks. Was it really worth it – even for a sort of immortality?

She smiled slightly. She had a sort of immortality already, in a roundabout way. Even if she died, here and now – which, obviously, she wasn't planning on doing for a moment – in just under 2,000 years she'd be back on Earth, wandering about London, growing up. Almost 200,000 years after that, she'd be on a space station, defeating the Daleks. More years than she could comprehend after that, she'd be watching the Earth die.

But although that was the future, it was her past. And right now she should be concentrating on her present. What was happening to her?

She suddenly jerked herself awake. She hadn't been asleep exactly, but she'd got totally caught up in her thoughts, started to drift off. That wine must have relaxed her a bit too much! She remembered that time with Shareen, when they were both kids, when they'd planned to sneak out to Danny Fennel's party and had half-inched a bottle of wine from her mum's kitchen cupboard to get them pepped up ready. Except after a glass each they'd fallen asleep, and they not only missed the party but got the ticking-off of the century from Jackie as well.

Rose blinked. She wasn't ten any more, and it'd take more than a glass of Lambrusco to make her nod off these days. So why was she suddenly feeling so sleepy?

She forced her head up and caught sight of Ursus. He was sitting on a bench just watching her, and his expression made her feel all hollow inside. Suddenly, it was *Silence of the Lambs* time. How could she have been so stupid? They'd had suspicions he was a nutter, hadn't they, and yet still she had merrily stepped into his fly-trapping parlour because of some stupid idea about having to avoid the paradox that would occur if the statue was never made.

Ursus rose and approached her. He eased the wine cup from her unresisting hand and Rose realised the truth as he waved it in front of her face. He'd drugged the wine. And she'd made it all so easy for him. She felt a sudden sick fear inside.

Ursus put down the cup and fetched a spear from the pile of godly odds and ends in the corner. Was this it? Was he going to stab her to death? Rose made a desperate effort to move, but her limbs had gone totally numb.

But he didn't stab her. Instead he prised open her hand and put the spear in it. What?

Rose tried to take advantage of this surprising situation – her captor having handed her a weapon! She tried once again to move, to thrust the pointed spearhead towards Ursus's ugly, gloating face.

But once again she failed.

Ursus pulled her from the bench. She tried to resist him

but she just couldn't. Now he was moving her helpless limbs, manipulating her as if she was a shop dummy from Henrik's.

Aside from being terrifying, it was totally humiliating. Rose Tyler, Barbie doll.

Had there ever been a Warrior Barbie? Because now, adding confusion to the terror and humiliation, Ursus had picked up a metal helmet from the pile and was placing it oh-so-carefully on her head.

This wasn't right. Her statue hadn't worn a helmet, hadn't held a spear. What was going on?

Ursus finally stopped treating her as if she was made of Plasticine. Rose couldn't see herself but she could feel that her head was held high, her spear clutched heroically in one hand as she stood tall and proud. So... what happened next?

The sculptor stood back, admiring her. It was an impersonal, clinical look; there was nothing in it that said she was a human being. She was nothing more to him than clay to be moulded into shape.

She tried to speak again. Her fear, her desperation, must have given her strength, because the slightest of slight sounds came out, something that might just have been recognised as 'Nooooo'.

Ursus frowned. 'Don't do that,' he said.

That was good – wasn't it? At least he had spoken to her. Anything you could do to make them see you as a person, that was the thing.

Suddenly he turned his back on Rose, and she felt a stab of hope. He'd changed his mind, he wasn't going to do anything to her...

But he just walked over to the covered shape in the

corner. Grasping the sheet, he pulled it off, revealing what was below.

It was a statue, as Rose had suspected. A man with wings on his hat and his shoes, like on the Interflora logo. But there was something familiar about him… The curled hair, the handsome features – surely this was Tiro? But he'd said he hadn't even started modelling yet.

Ursus smiled at the statue. 'He didn't make things difficult for me,' he said. 'He knew that beauty is more important than life.'

Rose's stomach seemed to vanish inside her. This couldn't really be happening to her. It was a dream, one of those ones where your legs won't obey you, where you can't run, however hard you try. The talking cats had been real and everything since had been a dream – a nightmare.

But it didn't seem as if the nightmare was ever going to end.

The Doctor had spent the morning doing his Sherlock Holmes thing, not that he thought there was much else to be discovered here. Rose, he hoped, would be using her own detective instincts to find things out from Ursus, while he'd drawn a blank in his search around the estate. Gracilis had suggested having the slaves tortured to make sure they were telling the truth, but the Doctor had managed to persuade him out of that.

The more people he spoke to, the more convinced he became that only Ursus had any answers. After sharing a lunch of bread and cheese with Gracilis, the Doctor decided that he needed to find out if Rose had discovered anything. Taking some food with him as an excuse – after all, surely even an artist's model was allowed lunch – he headed over to Ursus's workshop.

As the Doctor neared the stable yard, a cart was just pulling away. In the back of it he could see a large wrapped object nestling in a bed of straw. Never one to ignore even the least suspicious of circumstances, he jogged after the cart and jumped on the back before it had gone 100 yards.

'Hoy!' cried the carter.

'Don't mind me!' called back the Doctor. 'Just wanted a quick look at what you're carrying here.'

He began to unwrap the object – the human-sized object.

The carter pulled up and jumped down. 'What do you think you're doing? I was told to come here, pick up the goods and deliver 'em,' he said, coming round to the back. 'If that arrives damaged, it's me who'll get the blame.'

'That assumes I'm going to be damaging it,' said the Doctor. 'And I haven't the slightest intention of harming this – aha! This charming statue – of Mercury, messenger of the gods, if his winged hat is anything to go by.'

He rewrapped the sculpture, patted it on its draped head and hopped off the back of the cart, just as the carter was heaving himself onto it.

'Now, don't let me hold you up any further,' said the Doctor. 'I'm sure you're a very busy man – course you are, statues don't deliver themselves, do they?' He waved a gracious hand in the direction of the road, and the carter smiled, despite himself.

But as the Doctor walked back towards the estate, he wasn't smiling. He'd recognised the statue. Yes, it was Mercury – but it was modelled on a living man, and that man was the slave Tiro.

But there was no way Ursus could have completed the

statue of Tiro already. No way on earth.

The most terrible thought struck the Doctor. A thought that explained why Ursus was able to complete statues so quickly. Why they were so lifelike. Why his tools were unused and his workshop unsullied by marble dust.

The Doctor began to run.

Ursus walked back to frozen Rose. With the gloved tips of one hand, he grasped the gloved tips of the other. He pulled. Slowly, teasingly, the glove came off and he let it flop to the floor – a gross, terrifying striptease. Then he took the ends of the remaining glove in his teeth and pulled that off too.

'All my life, all I have wanted to do was to create beauty. But the gods cursed me with these…'

He held up his huge, stubby-fingered hands. They were white, flabby, not the calloused tools of a craftsman.

'I was taunted and teased for years, but I did not give up. I made vows to my goddess, promising sacrifices if she gave me what I desired. And then, one day – she did. I told her what I wished for most – the ability to make beauty in stone. And she granted me my desire.'

Slowly, oh so slowly, he moved closer to Rose, hands raised.

'I have fame now, renown. I am pitied no longer. My mother holds her head up high and talks with pride about "my son". I have money, money to buy all I want, money to revenge myself on those who once mocked me. But most of all… I have beauty. I can create beauty.'

He reached out a hand to Rose, as if he was going to stroke her cheek.

She had a memory: a man lying in a hospital bed. Petrifold regression, the Doctor had called that. Had she caught petrifold regression? Had Ursus given it to her? *What was happening to her?*

The last thing she saw was the horn of plenty, still lying unheeded and unwanted in the corner of the room.

The Doctor skidded to a halt in front of the stables. There was another cart there, an empty one this time, standing ready to receive its load. He was just contemplating the locked door when he heard a sound from the other side of it – grunting, groaning, the squeak of wheels. The door swung open and there was Ursus, pulling a wheeled pallet with a marble figure on it. The statue was lying horizontal and the Doctor couldn't see what it was, but he had a pretty good idea.

He launched himself on the sculptor. 'What have you done to Rose?'

Ursus was as strong as his bear namesake, but the Doctor's anger made him a match for any man. They grappled, falling to the floor and rolling over and over. As the Doctor lay on the ground, he spotted Vanessa creeping up towards them, a bronze lamp in her hands. She raised it above her head…

'That's it, Vanessa!' shouted the Doctor as he twisted round, gaining the upper hand again…

And everything went black.

The Doctor rubbed his sore head and sat up. He sneezed – a piece of hay was sticking up his nose. A donkey looked at him curiously. He was in a stable. Someone must have dragged him here. He looked around.

Crouched beside a pillar, trembling slightly, he could see Vanessa staring at him. She shrank away as he climbed to his feet.

'I… I'm sorry,' she squeaked, more mouse-like than ever.

'You hit me,' the Doctor said, coldly and angrily. 'You stopped me from rescuing Rose.'

'I didn't mean to!' She was almost crying. 'You moved! I meant to hit Ursus!'

The Doctor narrowed his eyes. 'Say I believe you – for now. Where is Rose? Where did he take her?'

'I didn't see Rose!' she gasped. 'Only a statue.'

The Doctor let that pass. 'Well, where is Ursus now?' he demanded.

'I… I don't know,' the girl stammered.

'I think you do,' said the Doctor. 'I think you know a lot more than you're letting on, *Vanessa*. Like, what's Hadrian's Wall, Vanessa?'

She looked at him, wide-eyed and terrified.

'Well?' he said.

She could barely get the words out. 'It's a wall. It divides England from Scotland.'

The Doctor raised an eyebrow. 'A wall that's not been built yet, dividing two places that won't be named for a few hundred years?'

Vanessa burst into tears.

'You know, I was suspicious the instant you were introduced,' the Doctor continued. '"Vanessa". Sounds quite Roman, I admit. Marcia, Claudia, Julia, Vanessa… But I happen to know, because I'm extremely clever, that the name was invented in the eighteenth century by a writer chap called Jonathan Swift. And there you were, a girl with a name from years in the future, sitting at a table working out Merik's Theorem. Oh, I know what astrological calculations look like, and I know what Merik's Theorem looks like, and that was definitely the latter, not the former. So would you like to tell me what a girl from at least the twenty-fourth century is doing in the second century AD, and –' he leaned over and shouted at her – 'what has happened to Rose!'

Vanessa looked up at him through her tears. Then slowly, shakily, she pulled a small black tube out of a fold in her coarse woollen tunic. Her finger hovered over the red button at one end as she pointed it straight at the Doctor. 'Let me go – or I'll shoot!'

SIX

The Doctor flung his hands up in the air. 'Don't shoot! Please don't shoot! I'm begging you!'

Vanessa looked confused as he threw himself onto his knees in front of her.

'For pity's sake, don't shoot!' he cried.

Her hand wavered – and the Doctor reached up and plucked the device from her. 'Thank you,' he said. 'Confuse the enemy, that's the trick. Not that I'm saying you're necessarily an enemy. I mean, I don't think you would really have shot me.' He glanced down at the device in his hand. 'Especially not with a vid-caster remote control.'

She gave him a faint, shaky smile. 'It's the only thing I've got from home. I was holding it when…' She trailed off and a tear trickled down her cheek.

The Doctor jumped to his feet and Vanessa flinched away from him. He sank down on the hay beside her and put a kindly arm around her shoulder. 'Y'see, I know for a fact you come from the twenty-fourth century,' he said, holding up the remote control. 'This proves it. So, are you going to tell me about it?'

She shook her head and the Doctor could feel her tensing

up. He dropped his arm back to his side.

'Look, I'm sorry I shouted at you,' he continued. 'I'm just upset about Rose. After all, I suspect that whatever has happened to her is what happened to Optatus a week ago, and you didn't have anything to do with that – well, unless you're playing a very elaborate game with a lot of accomplices. If this was a detective story I'd probably have to consider that – but it isn't, and while I may not have a twirly moustache, I can still tell a genuinely scared person when I see one. You were really scared back at that apartment, weren't you?'

She nodded, but the tension was still evident in her whole body. For what seemed like the first time, she began to speak, really speak – a human being, not a frightened sheep. 'I've been scared for such a long time now. I was so frightened and confused when I arrived here. There was some sort of festival going on, people everywhere. Balbus rescued me, gave me food and drink. But I said something – I don't even remember what – and I got it wrong. He jumped to the conclusion I could tell the future.'

'Which you could,' said the Doctor. 'Very accurately.'

'Well, yes. And then he accused me of being a runaway slave and said I'd be executed – unless I worked for him. And so I had to. I did my best. I'd read horoscopes in magazines and I've studied astronomy. I thought it would keep me safe, until...'

The Doctor looked hard at her. 'Until what?'

She gave a half-smile. 'Until I could get home.' The smile went. 'But it was terrible. I don't know my history well enough. I was warning people to stay away from Pompeii, but apparently that happened years ago. And I worried that if I said a word about future emperors I'd get executed for treason. And then there were people like your friend Gracilis, who desperately needed hope and help, and I was giving them lies, feeding on their misery. All the while Balbus looked on, getting richer and richer from the things I was saying.'

'The prophet's profits,' quipped the Doctor.

She smiled again. 'And then you and Rose arrived. I knew at once you weren't ordinary Romans.'

The Doctor gave a modest shrug. 'Well, I must admit that I make heads turn wherever I go. It's a burden that I just have to live with.'

'I was scared again, of who you might be, but I was so desperate to get away from Balbus... And then Rose talked to me, and she seemed so nice, but I couldn't bring myself to tell her anything, just in case...' She gazed up at the Doctor with pleading eyes. 'Can you take me home?' she said. 'Please?'

'Where is home?' the Doctor asked her. 'Where – and when?'

Vanessa took a deep breath. 'I'm from Earth – actually Sardinia, so I'm really quite close – in everything but years. When I left, it was 2375.'

The Doctor darted a look at her. He knew that on Earth, in Sardinia, in 2375, they didn't have time travel. So that was yet another mystery.

'And how exactly did you come to be in Rome, AD 120, instead? Something a bit more than a wrong turn on the way home from school, I'm guessing.'

The girl didn't so much try to evade the question as ignore it altogether. 'Can you take me home?' she said again.

The Doctor decided not to pursue the matter for now.

He shook his head. 'Not yet,' he said. 'Not until I find Rose.'

'But she must still be in the studio,' Vanessa told him. 'I've been watching all morning and she hasn't left.'

The Doctor knew that wasn't the case. But he allowed himself to hope, just for a moment. 'All right,' he said. 'Let's look.'

The workshop door was still open. They searched every room – but there was nothing. No Rose, no Tiro, no statues, no marble dust. The Doctor dived upon a scrap of papyrus that was lying on a table, but all it said, in hard-to-read cursive script, was 'One statue to Rome', followed by a figure – a receipt from the carter? He flung it down.

'I don't understand,' said Vanessa. 'Where is she?'

'I don't know!' The Doctor's worst fears were being confirmed, and he couldn't hide from the conclusion any longer. 'The statue Ursus had – did you see it?'

'Yes,' she said. 'It was a statue of Rose.'

'Which isn't possible.' He was almost shaking with shock and anger.

Vanessa held out a nervous hand to comfort him, but the Doctor threw it off. 'What is it?' she said, scared.

'That wasn't a statue of Rose. That was Rose herself. That was Rose in the museum.' The Doctor stood petrified for a moment, as if he'd been turned to stone too. Then he drew himself up to his full height, towering over Vanessa. Wouldn't give in to the fear; would never give in. 'We're going to find her,' he said.

He told Vanessa to wait while he went back to his room, where there was something he needed. Right at the moment he couldn't think how the sonic screwdriver would help, but he needed any possible advantage he could get.

The screwdriver was where he'd left it, but there was something else there too, something made of cloth. He picked it up: it was a small drawstring purse, just the right size for a sonic screwdriver. There was a note too:

Dear Doctor

Happy unbirthday! Bet you didn't know I could sew. Marcia showed me what to do.

Love Rose

The Doctor crumpled the note in his hand, overcome with grief and anger and helplessness. Then he carefully tied the pouch to his belt and set off to find his friend.

Vanessa hurried to catch up with the Doctor as he strode out of the house and made his way to the path that led from the villa's entrance to the road. Here and there the path was muddy, and cart tracks could be seen. The Doctor set off, following them.

'Shouldn't we… tell someone?' asked Vanessa, out of breath from the pace the Doctor was setting.

'No time,' said the Doctor abruptly, not slowing down.

But soon he had to stop. The path had joined with the main road. It was a typical Roman road, long and straight. And as everyone knew, all roads led to Rome. What people didn't always mention was that this meant all roads also led away from Rome.

The Doctor flung himself on his hands and knees, looking for tracks. 'Here,' he said after a minute. 'A cart turned to the left.'

But Vanessa had been searching too. 'I think one turned to the right,' she said.

The Doctor got up and joined her. 'Damn!' he said. 'We've got to find a place where the tracks cross. Find out which one came first.'

But their search proved fruitless.

'Right!' said the Doctor suddenly, springing to his feet in the middle of examining a dry and definitely trackless bit of road for the third time. 'We'll have to divide our resources.'

Vanessa looked worried.

'I mean,' the Doctor explained, 'you go one way and I'll go the other. Look for clues. Talk to people. Find out anything you can.' He glanced up into the sky, shading his eyes. 'Wait till the sun's got down to about – there,' he said, pointing. 'Then head back and meet me here.'

'But… which way do I go?'

The Doctor thought for a second. 'Rose and I arrived on the Ides of March. That means –' he counted on his fingers – 'it's almost the Quinquatrus. Yes, Balbus mentioned that. A festival that celebrates Minerva's birthday on 19 March. Which makes her a Pisces,' he added with a grin. 'And Minerva is—'

'Goddess of art and artisans,' completed Vanessa, catching on.

'It's the time when all her devotees bring offerings,' continued the Doctor. 'And I don't mean a bunch of daffs or a box of Milk Tray. If I remember correctly, they gather at her temple on the Aventine Hill. So, Ursus could be taking her there.'

Vanessa nodded. 'Yes, that makes sense. So he's taken Rose to Rome.'

But the Doctor shook his head. 'Not so fast. There were two carts and they've gone in two different directions. And we found what is probably a receipt from the carter – to take a statue to Rome. So it could be the *other* cart that's gone there.' He spun on the spot, eyes closed and one arm stretched out. Stopping, he opened his eyes and found he was pointing to the right – towards Rome. 'I'll go this way, you go that way. OK?'

But he didn't give her time to answer. He was already heading off, jogging down the road that led to Rome.

The sun crept across the sky and the Doctor met nobody. The weather was warm for March – perhaps everyone was having an afternoon siesta. Every now and again he spotted cart tracks – but that didn't mean a thing, they could belong to any cart. Giving up was not in his nature, but hopeless plans weren't either. He'd return to the villa, see if Vanessa had had any luck; talk to Gracilis – beg the loan of a cart, or a carriage, or even just a donkey.

He stared fruitlessly into the distance for a final second, as if Rose would somehow be revealed to him. Then he turned and headed back.

The Doctor beat Vanessa; there was no sign of her either at the road's edge or on the path to the villa. He was making for the main entrance when he spotted a flash of white among the trees. Optatus's statue.

His hearts felt heavy. Optatus's 'statue'.

He made his way towards the grove and wasn't really surprised to find Gracilis and Marcia there. They smiled sadly up at him.

'You must think us sentimental fools, Doctor,' said Gracilis. 'But it helps us feel he is still with us.'

The Doctor nodded. He moved over to the statue and looked at it carefully. Then he ran a gentle hand down its right arm. 'There's a bump,' he said. 'Just here.'

Marcia looked. 'Optatus broke his arm,' she said. 'He fell from a tree. The surgeon set it, but it didn't heal quite right.'

'Amazing for Ursus to pay such attention to detail...' said the Doctor; a hint. But he didn't continue. Couldn't let them know the truth.

He stood for a moment, silently gazing at the statue. Then he said abruptly, 'Rose has disappeared. She's in deadly danger. We might already be too late.'

Gracilis gasped, and Marcia looked as though she was about to faint clean away.

The Doctor carried on, 'I think she's on her way to Rome. Gracilis, can you help me get there?'

Gracilis nodded eagerly.

The Doctor turned to Marcia. 'Vanessa is helping me to search. But I can't wait any longer for her. When she gets back, will you send word by messenger to let me know what she's discovered?'

Marcia also nodded.

'Then there's no time to lose,' said the Doctor. 'Let's go.'

Not for the first time, the Doctor cursed the fact that the TARDIS was sitting somewhere in a Roman back street, well over a day's journey away by donkey. Gracilis had insisted on coming with him, so the Doctor had had to wait impatiently while he bade farewell to his wife and collected provisions. Some people seemed totally unaware that the smallest second could mean the difference between life and death.

Gracilis still hoped to find a clue in Rome as to Optatus's whereabouts. The Doctor didn't tell him that the best clue was right there at his own villa. He did eventually say that he suspected Ursus was responsible for Rose's plight. But more than that he did not reveal.

Every now and again the Doctor would jump out of the carriage to check for wheel marks, or to ask a plodding peasant a question, but none of the answers enlightened him. As darkness fell, they approached a way station, where the Doctor had no intention of spending the night.

Gracilis protested. He was as eager as the Doctor to reach Rome, but the donkeys had to rest.

'Then I'll carry on by foot,' the Doctor declared.

'But perhaps Ursus is resting here too,' suggested Gracilis, stopping the Doctor in his tracks for a moment.

The Doctor resumed walking – but now his footsteps were bent towards the guesthouse. 'All right. We'll have it your way,' he said.

They went inside, and the Doctor immediately cornered the proprietor and described Ursus to him. The man claimed not to have seen the sculptor, however many times the Doctor asked.

Gracilis called for wine, while the Doctor paced the room.

The Doctor suddenly had a thought. 'You're a way station. You must have donkeys here. Or, even better, horses,' he said to the proprietor.

The man bowed obsequiously. 'Indeed we do, sir.'

'Then I'd like to hire your best horse, please, immediately.'

The man humbly begged the Doctor's pardon, but feared that such a thing was not possible. 'I'm afraid our beasts are not fresh and would not be fit to undertake a long journey.'

The Doctor scowled but, reining in his impatience, finally agreed to sit down and share a meal with Gracilis.

Just as they were finishing, there was a sound of hoof

beats from outside and a few moments later the door was flung open. A haughty-looking man in his forties entered, Roman nose stuck high in the air. He clicked his fingers and, as the proprietor hurried over, relieved a slave of the cup of wine that was heading towards Gracilis.

Gracilis began to bristle, his chest puffing out in indignation, but the Doctor raised a hand to stall his angry words.

'Hello,' he said cheerfully, jumping up and offering a hand to the newcomer, 'you look a bit thirsty. Long journey?'

The man stared at the Doctor in disdain, taking in his plain tunic, distinctly un-Roman sideburns and not-at-all-subservient grin. He did not shake hands.

'I am Lucius Aelius Rufus. I have travelled from Gaul on business for the emperor,' he said impressively.

Gracilis jumped slightly. Clearly he'd heard of the man.

'Gaul, eh?' said the Doctor. 'Ooh, rough place. Nice scenery, though.'

Rufus ignored him. 'I wait here merely while my horse is changed, then I will be on my way.'

The Doctor pricked up his ears. 'Your horse?' he said. 'I'm afraid you're out of luck. No fresh horses here.'

'Nonsense,' said Rufus. 'It has all been arranged.' The Doctor turned to stare at the proprietor. The unfortunate man cringed like Uriah Heep and begged the Doctor's pardon again. They had received word that this gentleman was coming. The last horse had been reserved for him. The proprietor was so sorry if his earlier words had misled the Doctor, no disrespect had been intended.

'I see, I see,' said the Doctor mildly, taking a seat opposite Rufus and ignoring his unwelcoming stare. 'You must be on very important business if you can't even rest for the night,' he said.

'Of course.' The newcomer sounded bored.

'Life or death, great benefit to mankind, that sort of thing?'

'My business is my own,' Rufus said, and turned his head away in a vain attempt to stop the Doctor addressing him.

'But you would tell me if it were life or death?' the Doctor persisted.

The man's hand clenched angrily around his cup as he drained his wine. He said nothing.

'Well, I'll take that as read, then,' said the Doctor.

He stood up and walked over to Gracilis. 'Catch me up if you can, and make sure he doesn't have the stablehands beaten,' he whispered in his friend's ear. Then he casually wandered out of the front door, leaving Gracilis looking bemusedly after him.

A few minutes later, the sound of hoof beats could be heard from the road outside the guesthouse, gradually fading into the distance. It took Rufus a moment to cotton on, and by the time he had followed the Doctor out, horse and rider were just a spot in the distance.

SEVEN

The Doctor arrived in Rome during the morning of the 19th – the Quinquatrus – and made his way through the streets to the Aventine Hill. He'd not passed Ursus's cart during his night-time ride, nor found any trace of him at guesthouses along the way, but he wasn't letting that discourage him – he was hoping that the man was already in Rome. First stop was the temple of Minerva – the patron of artists. There was a crowd outside when he arrived and the Doctor moved through it, chatting as he went.

'Minerva's great, isn't she?' he kept saying to various worshippers. 'And by the way, you're arty sorts, do you happen to know the sculptor Ursus at all?'

But none of them did. Oh, they knew of him – but Ursus clearly wasn't the life-and-soul-of-the-artistic-community type. He didn't join in the gossip or swap tips; he wouldn't recommend suppliers or train apprentices. His sculpting abilities were praised – but his meteoric rise to fame hadn't gone down that well. The glory he'd received in less than a year was not appreciated by those who had been serving their apprenticeships for many moons. They told of tantrums and threats, of snubs and sneers.

So, the Doctor found out quite a lot about Ursus – but not his location.

Refusing to be disheartened, he began a whirlwind tour of Rome. Any watcher would be hard put to decide if he was the most devout of men, visiting each temple in turn, or the most irreverent, bringing no offerings and showing little regard for custom. The Doctor also visited taverns and snack bars, demonstrating an indefatigable appetite for honeyed wine, hot pies and gossip. 'I know a statue by Ursus,' someone would say, and the Doctor would hare off across the city to find a marble Vesta or Flora – some astoundingly lifelike creation that filled the Doctor with fury. He was as certain as he could be of the nature of Ursus's true 'talent'. No sculptor could have created this many works of art in less than a year with just a hammer and chisel.

The evening was drawing in and the Doctor was no closer to finding Ursus, or Rose, or any clue at all. But he wouldn't stop looking.

Then he spotted a shrine he hadn't visited yet. It was small, not like some of the magnificent temples he'd seen earlier, but it was a shrine to Fortuna herself. Where better to find a statue of Fortuna than in her own temple? Surely the goddess of fortune must bring him luck!

There were no priests around – his first lucky break. The Doctor took a deep breath and stepped inside.

A statue of Fortuna stood at the end of the shrine and his hearts quickened. But although she shared a pose with the statue they'd seen in the British Museum, although she carried a cornucopia and gazed proudly forward, this was not Rose – was not even a new statue. The marble was discoloured, the paint faded.

'Rose is prettier than you,' the Doctor told the statue.

'Thanks,' said the statue.

Of course it wasn't the statue. It was a voice coming from somewhere behind it. But all the same, there was something wrong here. The Doctor started forward to investigate, but as he did so he almost trod on a small glass phial that came rolling out from behind the statue. It seemed to be full of some bright green substance. He stooped to pick it up, as the voice continued, 'This'll bring Rose back to life – and the others. All praise to me – that is, Fortuna, and all that.'

The Doctor took another determined step towards the statue, but a door slammed open behind him and a voice yelled breathlessly, 'Doctor! Doctor!'

He turned to see Gracilis stumbling in. 'Thank goodness I've found you!' he puffed. 'I've come to warn you –'

But there was another interruption. Into the shrine strode Lucius Aelius Rufus, the man from the guesthouse, accompanied by several armed guards.

'There he is!' roared Rufus, pointing at the Doctor.

The Doctor looked back towards the statue, still puzzled – but then turned to face Rufus's men as they came forward and grabbed him.

'Well, excuse me,' said the Doctor, mildly scolding. 'This is no way to behave in a temple. I think it might be what they call sacrilege. Or is it blasphemy – I never can remember the difference? One of them, anyway, is what it is.'

The men ignored him and started to drag him towards the door.

'So, where are we going?' the Doctor asked conversationally.

Rufus smiled, showing a gold tooth. 'To the arena,' he said.

The Doctor smiled back. 'A day out!' he said. 'That's a nice thought. Tell you what, though, I'd be just as happy with an intimate little dinner for two, bit of a chat…'

One of the men slapped him across the face, and the Doctor stumbled. To his horror, the glass phial fell from his hand. He tried to pull away but the men were strong and he was dizzy from the blow. 'Gracilis!' he tried to call, but they were out of the shrine now and he received another slap for his troubles.

Not only was he being dragged into danger, but he was being dragged further and further away from what might be Rose's salvation. And he was unable to investigate the biggest mystery of the day – why was someone in an ancient Roman temple talking to him through something that sounded distinctly like a vocoder?

It was soon only too clear where the Doctor was being taken. An enormous structure loomed up ahead, a giant round building that was as tall as thirty Doctors, made of gleaming white stone that sharply reminded him of Rose's probable fate. Dozens of archways stretched round the lowest storey, currently devoid of life. But the Doctor knew that at times tens of thousands of people would stream through those entrances, eager to see the bloody spectacle that awaited beyond.

This was the Flavian Amphitheatre, which would one day become known as the Colosseum. Home to gladiator fights, wild beast hunts, and thousands upon thousands of grisly executions.

'Are we going to take in a show?' asked the Doctor with interest. 'Only we seem to have come on the wrong day. It's a bit quiet, so probably better to come back another time.'

'No blood is shed on the Quinquatrus,' one of his captors informed him.

'Ah, righto, pleased to hear it. Well, if you'll just let me go, then…'

The man grinned unpleasantly. 'Tomorrow, on the other hand, when we honour Mars…'

The Doctor sighed. He was getting tired of this. Suddenly he put on the brakes, digging in his heels and making his surprised captors unbalance. He brought his arms down sharply, wrenched them round and broke the men's grips, leaving them gaping in astonishment.

'Don't worry, gents, I can find my own way home,' he said, moving rapidly out of their reach…

…and into the arms of two other men who had come up behind him.

This was really not his lucky day after all.

Coins changed hands between the two lots of men and the Doctor was dragged off again, this time through a door and down into a dark, malodorous underground structure.

The two men who held him fitted the place well. One was short and stout, a curved scar bisecting his cheek from mouth to eye, giving him a twisted clown's leer. The other was taller, with a long face crowned by greasy black hair. Both smelled of sweat and misery.

The Doctor recognised his surroundings – not as a specific, but as the sort of place he'd visited involuntarily hundreds upon hundreds of times. The damp walls, the gloom, the tang of fear – this was a dungeon.

'I haven't had a trial, you know,' he remarked conversationally to the scarred man, who was referred to by his colleague as Thermus.

'Tried in your absence,' the man replied.

'Really? You know, last time I looked, the penalty for borrowing a horse wasn't death. I realise I may be terribly behind the times – or possibly ahead of them – but I would have thought a "sorry, bit of a misunderstanding, here's a *denarius* or two for your troubles" was more to the point.'

'We don't make the law,' said the tall man, Flaccus.

'No, but Lucius Aelius Rufus does,' Thermus pointed out.

Both men seemed to find this observation the height of wit and snorted happily.

'Ah,' said the Doctor. 'Am I to believe that the gentleman in question is a magistrate of some kind? The corrupt, power-hungry kind with an inflated sense of his own importance, perhaps?'

The men chortled, which the Doctor took as a 'yes'.

'I need to see someone else, then,' he told them. 'Someone who can overrule Rufus. The emperor. If I could just get an audience with the emperor…'

By now the Doctor's captors were laughing so hard they were finding it hard to stay upright.

'See… the… emperor!' gasped Flaccus. 'Yeah, we'll send him a note. He's always popping round of an evening.'

'Well, that's handy, then,' said the Doctor. 'Oh, hang on, were you being sarcastic? Because obviously that's enormously helpful. Tell me, did you receive any training in the social-work aspect of your role here, or did it just come naturally?'

They'd reached the end of a corridor lit only by a single guttering torch. The flames flickered on metal bars ahead, a tinsel sparkle among the gloom. Thermus dropped the Doctor's arm and moved forward, a large metal key in his hand. The door swung open.

Flaccus grabbed hold of the pouch at the Doctor's belt and tore it off.

'No!' cried the Doctor.

'Yes,' said Flaccus sarcastically. 'After all, it's no more use to you.' Then he gave an almighty shove and the Doctor stumbled forward into the cell.

'This is a complete miscarriage of justice!'

But they took no notice. Thermus slammed the door and the key turned.

Normally, the Doctor would not have been concerned. Any lock could be undone by his sonic screwdriver. But that was the sonic screwdriver that was in his belt pouch. And that was the belt pouch – Rose's belt pouch – that was on the other side of the bars, gradually retreating out of sight as it swung from Thermus's sweaty, podgy hand.

The Doctor turned from the bars and realised for the first time that he was not alone. Eyes were caught in the flickering light, reflecting out of unseen faces: a cartoon for Hallowe'en. He walked further in and could see the eyes' owners better – a sea of hopeless faces barely registering his presence. He sat down on the cold stone floor and smiled around, although it was doubtful if anyone would care, even if they could see him. 'Hello,' he said. 'I'm the Doctor.'

There was silence for a moment, then a voice out of the murk said, 'Can you cure crucifixion, then?'

'Yeah, or being burnt alive?' said another.

'Prevention is better than cure, don't you think?' the Doctor said evenly.

There were discontented murmurs at this.

A more reasonable voice spoke. 'Look, we're all going to

die tomorrow. No way out of it. Most of us even chose this way to go.'

'Better a quick death than a slow one in the mines,' a fourth voice put in.

'Yeah. So forgive us if we're not that welcoming. Not much point in making friends when you might have to kill that person tomorrow.'

'Oh, I don't know,' said the Doctor. 'I don't think making friends can ever be a bad thing, can it? It's not like I'm expecting you to toss round a beanbag and tell an interesting fact about yourselves. Let's just have a chat. For example, why are you going to be killing each other tomorrow?'

There were a few disbelieving snorts from his audience.

'Are you thick or what?'

'He must be a foreigner,' said the kinder voice.

'Look, mate, that's the way it is here. We don't know exactly how we're gonna go, but we're gonna go. Burnt alive, crucified, fed to the beasts – or made to fight each other to the death. And then the only way you'll survive is to kill and kill again and keep killing, in the desperate hope that the crowd'll be so impressed they won't want you to be finished off in the end. It's the only chance you'll have of getting out of there alive.'

'Seems a very small chance.'

'Right. But better than no chance at all.'

The Doctor's voice was full of sadness. 'Where there's life there's hope? How can I tell you that's wrong?' He paused. 'But what about dignity? What about not participating willingly in this bloody charade? What about all standing together and refusing to fight?'

'Then we get cut down where we stand. No life, definitely

no hope. No one's ever escaped from the arena.'

The Doctor smiled, though none of his companions could see it. 'Then it's your lucky day. Because doing things that no one's ever done is my speciality.'

The Doctor came to think of his four chatty cell mates as John, Paul, George and Ringo. There were others too, men and women, freemen and slaves, too far into the depths of despair to talk to anyone. Several hundred prisoners were being held ready for the next day's games. Many of them had been a willing audience at previous games and knew just what to expect.

'You never want 'em to go free,' confessed George. 'That's not how it works. Everyone's howling for their blood, and you howl too.'

'I remember this brilliant one,' said Paul. 'There was this bloke, a musician, and he thought he was there to play to the crowd. Then halfway through some tune they let the animals out! He thought it was a mistake and he's running around, trying to get them to let him out, but of course they don't. So he tries charming the beasts with his playing, like he's Orpheus in the Underworld!'

'Did it work?' asked John.

'Nah. Reckon the lion what got him wasn't much of a music lover.'

John chipped in with his own anecdote. 'There was this time when they'd got a couple of blind men,' he said. 'Gave them both swords and set them at it. They're swinging away, no idea what's going on, occasionally getting a bit of ear or something by luck. That was hilarious.' He paused. 'Doesn't seem so funny now.'

'It doesn't, does it?' Paul concurred.

George and Ringo muttered their agreement too.

'Then let's talk about the alternatives,' said the Doctor.

Some of the prisoners drifted off to sleep, but the Doctor stayed awake all night. Occasionally guards would visit, and the Doctor took every opportunity to remind them that he was, in his opinion, there unlawfully. They only laughed.

Even the Doctor, with his excellent time sense, found it hard to tell when the next day came. Night reigned eternally in the dungeon, the single torch outside functioning as both sun and moon. It was sounds rather than light that alerted them all: roars and howls and bellows.

'Getting ready for the wild beast hunt,' explained George. 'First business of the day.' Having assumed the Doctor to be a stranger to Rome, he'd taken it on himself to explain all the customs of the arena. 'Marvellous animals they've got. You being from foreign parts, you might have seen some of the beasts already, though, back home.'

'Leopards they've got, and stags, and these incredible tall things called giraffes.'

'And elephants, don't forget them.'

The Doctor clenched his fists. 'Do you know how many species will be made extinct by these games?' he demanded furiously. 'Good grief, what is it about you humans? You think you're the only thing on this planet that's worth anything, that you can ravage nature just to show your superiority. Can you even comprehend a fraction of what's being done here?' Then he calmed down just as quickly, became sorrowful instead of angry. 'No, you probably can't. And I expect you wouldn't care if you could.'

'He must be foreign,' Ringo concluded after a moment.

'Either that or barmy.'

'Foreign,' the others all agreed.

After a while, other sounds began to be heard, creeping faintly over the distance. There was music, followed by the cheering of an expectant crowd, growing in volume as more and more people arrived.

'They drive the beasts into cages,' George explained, 'and then they're hauled up to ground level. The arena's all set up with trees and hills and things, and the trainers use burning brands to force them out into it. They try to create a bit of panic, make the things run around for a while, and then they hunt 'em down. Some of the beasts kill each other, and that's all right, but the trainers finish the rest off. I've seen a man kill a tiger with his bare hands,' he concluded wistfully.

They sat in silence for a while, listening. Gradually the roars of the animals grew fewer and fewer, and the cheers of the crowd reached a peak.

'That's that,' observed John.

'What happens next?' the Doctor asked.

'Next? Well, first they have to clear away all the bodies. That's a bit of a job.'

'And then?'

'And then it's us. It's our time to die.'

EIGHT

The Doctor thumped his fist against the cell bars. 'All this for borrowing a horse. It's ridiculous!'

Ringo snorted. 'You think that's something? There's me, nice little business selling artworks, never said they were your genuine Greek, can't help what people thought, and then suddenly here I am about to go and meet Pluto.'

He'd obviously struck a chord. 'What they got me for's serious enough,' said George quietly. 'Only thing is, I didn't do it.' He paused in thought for a moment, then continued. 'Made the best pies in the city, I did. People came from miles around for one of my pies. Then one day this lad comes in. Posh sort, but looks like he's been in a fight, and he's barely able to stand from the drink. He's flashing his money bag around, so I give him a pie and ask him if he wants me to get a doctor. Next thing I know, he's on the floor. Dead.'

'I think I can guess what's coming,' said the Doctor.

George sniffed. 'They're all saying I poisoned him. Never mind that he barely touched his pie and he was half dead when he came in. Said I did it to get his money. Some toerag ran off with his purse while I was trying to bring him round. All my friends are saying I didn't do it. But his family were rich. So I didn't have a hope.'

'I'm sorry,' the Doctor murmured.

They sat there in silence for a moment. Then everyone froze as footsteps approached the dungeon cell. Everyone except the Doctor.

'Just try to remember what I said,' he told the others. 'If we stick together, who knows what we can achieve?'

'Well, for a start we can achieve death…' began Paul. 'Yeah, yeah, all right, it's worth a go.'

'Right!' called a voice as someone rattled the dungeon door.

A torch was pushed up to the bars, faintly illuminating the faces of the Doctor's four friends: bearded John, burly Paul, sad-eyed George and skinny Ringo. It also lit up the sneering face of Thermus, who was holding it. But his next words came as a surprise.

'Where's the bloke who kept on about being here illegally?'

The Doctor stood up and moved forward. 'Yes?' he said curtly. 'What do you want?'

He could just make out Thermus raising his eyebrows. 'There now, is that any way to talk to someone who's come to let you out?'

'Wouldn't have said it was, Thermus,' said Flaccus, standing beside him, holding the dungeon key. 'I'd have said that was more the way of an ungrateful wretch who doesn't appreciate all we've been doing for him.'

'What?' said the Doctor.

'You must have influential friends, sir,' continued Thermus, as the key was turned in the lock. 'We've been told it's all a big mistake and you're to be set free. I believe Rufus intends to apologise to you personally.'

Gracilis! thought the Doctor. He knew people in Rome, he must have arranged things. He felt a surge of gratitude towards the old man.

'Right. Well, good. I'll just have a few words with my friends—'

'No time for that, sir,' Flaccus told him. 'More than our job's worth to keep a man like you here with all of these criminals.'

Thermus took hold of the Doctor's arm and escorted him firmly, if rather more respectfully than before, out of the cell.

'Remember what I said!' the Doctor called back over his shoulder. 'Work together!'

The two guards led him through the dingy corridors. They passed an alcove in which stood a table with several flasks of wine and a few dice on it, obviously the guards' personal space. There was something else on the table too – a small cloth bag. The Doctor darted over and grabbed it.

'Mine, I think,' he said.

Thermus shrugged. The Doctor could tell by feel that they'd taken most of the coins he'd carried in it, but he wasn't going to start a fight over that. They'd left the sonic screwdriver, that was the main thing – he wondered what on earth they'd made of it.

They weren't retracing their steps from the night before; the Doctor was being led in a different direction now. The noise from the arena was getting louder and he thought with a pang of guilt about the men he'd just left behind. Despite his encouraging words to them, he knew it was unlikely that any of them would ever see their families again.

'Who arranged this?' he asked the guards. 'Was it Gracilis?'

'Gracilis?' said Thermus. 'Yes, I believe that was the name, wasn't it, Flaccus?'

'I think it was indeed,' said his colleague. 'He's been a good friend to you, that Gracilis.'

'He has,' said the Doctor.

'In fact, I think he's waiting just outside to meet you. Just up here, sir.' Flaccus indicated a ramp.

There was a door at the top.

The three of them walked up the ramp. Thermus opened the door – and, in an unpleasant echo of the night before, the Doctor found himself suddenly shoved through. As the door slammed behind him, he heard gales of laughter coming from the two guards.

Gracilis was not waiting to greet him.

No one was waiting to greet him – unless you counted the tens of thousands of cheering Roman citizens.

The Doctor was inside the arena.

The arena was huge, bigger than a football pitch. The floor was covered with fine white sand – to soak up the expected blood. Four tiers of seating held shouting Romans, a marble wall topped with a fence protecting the nearest spectators from the events occurring in front of them. The Doctor spotted the satisfied face of Lucius Aelius Rufus in the bottom row of seating.

The Time Lord's eyes flickered around the arena, searching for something – anything – that he could use to help himself. He could wield a sword with the best of them – but he had no sword. No weapon of any kind. Trees had been fixed in the arena floor and he ran over to one, not that he expected it would provide much protection from whatever he had to face.

There was a scream of delight from the crowd. A trapdoor had slammed open at the edge of the arena, followed by another and another. Slowly, reluctantly, animals were forced through the gaps. Lions, tigers, bears.

'Oh my!' said the Doctor, as the trapdoors slammed shut again.

The animals looked skinny and lethargic, half starved. They didn't want to attack, not yet. But the Doctor knew it wouldn't be long. There was still a scent of blood in the arena from the earlier mass slaughter, and it would make them look at him in a whole new way in a minute. And if there was any further reluctance, George had told him how the trainers – *bestiarii* – would soon be at hand with encouragement in the form of fire and weapons and raw meat.

The Doctor gave a bow to the crowd. They liked that and applauded. He turned to face Rufus. '*Nos morituri te salutamus,*' he called, although the salute he gave was probably not one the magistrate recognised. Nevertheless, the crowd applauded that too.

A lion was prowling closer, an old male whose once-magnificent mane now looked patchy and dull.

'You look tired,' the Doctor said softly to it. 'What life is this for you, the king of the jungle?' A thought struck him. 'I think what you really need is a sleep.' He reached into his belt pouch and pulled out the sonic screwdriver. A few twists and he pointed it at the approaching lion, which was now growling at him, deep in its throat.

He knew he shouldn't really use the sonic screwdriver, not in front of thousands upon thousands of primitive humans. But he was going to do it anyway. Not so much because he had to save himself, but because he still had to save Rose. And no one was going to stop him doing that.

There was a faint hum from the sonic screwdriver, but only the Doctor knew that it was producing another pitch too, a wave of sound inaudible to the human ear but which the lion would definitely pick up. And sure enough, the lion turned tail and slunk away. A few moments later it lay down on the ground, an elderly cat by the fireside.

There were cheers and jeers from the crowd – a few cheers at this strange man seeing off a lion with what looked like a tiny stick, but mainly jeers from those cheated of blood.

'Come on!' the Doctor called out to the audience. 'Did you really want it over so soon? Isn't the anticipation half the pleasure?'

Now a huge black bear was lumbering towards him.

'Hard to believe,' the Doctor told the bear, 'that teddy bears are so cute and you're so… not. No offence.'

He raised the sonic screwdriver again – but the bear did not stop. 'Ah,' said the Doctor. 'Make a note. Bears need a different frequency.'

The bear was getting faster now, obviously sensing prey. The Doctor leapt to the nearby tree and began to climb, nearing the top as the bear reached it. The bear stood on its hind legs and gripped the tree, shaking it.

'Note two,' said the Doctor. 'Bears are not put off by trees.'

He knew that if he jumped, the bear would be on him in a moment. Holding tightly on to the tree with one hand, he tried to adjust the settings on the sonic screwdriver with the other – but the bear gave the tree a massive shake and the device tumbled to the ground. And now the bear was beginning to climb the tree. It wasn't a big tree, probably wouldn't take its weight for long, but whether the bear caught him up high or when the tree collapsed wouldn't make all that much difference to the Doctor.

Slowly, carefully, he edged round the tree till he was directly above the bear. The creature flailed an angry paw upwards, still just out of reach. But any second now it would be there…

The Doctor jumped. Not onto the ground – but onto the bear's back. Startled, it dropped back to the ground, on all fours, and tried to shake him off. The Doctor held firm. The bear reared up onto its hind legs, roaring in agitation.

'Steady on, Ted,' the Doctor said. 'It's not easy being a "bear"-back rider, you know.'

The crowd loved this. It wasn't as good as a kill, but it tickled their fancy anyway, the slim young man treating this fierce creature as if it was a donkey or a mule.

The bear slammed back onto all four paws again. The Doctor tensed, wondering what its next move would be. Suddenly it swayed, ready to roll over and rub the irritation from its back. What to do? If he held on he'd be crushed, but if he let go the bear would be on him in a second…

The bear began to fall – and the Doctor spotted a gleam on the ground, out of the corner of his eye. He rolled with the creature, diving off at the very last moment and grabbing at the gleam. He rose with the sonic screwdriver in his hand, and as the bear righted itself and prepared to spring, he thrust it forward…

And the bear stopped. It gave a whine and began to back off, staring at the Doctor with hatred.

'Sorry,' the Doctor murmured.

But the crowd didn't like this. Two animals defeated and not a drop of blood spilt. If they couldn't have the Doctor's blood they'd settle for that of the beasts, but they weren't getting either.

Those in charge obviously sensed the mood of the crowd, knew that something had to happen soon. A door opened and two *bestiarii* came into the arena. One wielded a flaming torch, while the other held a trident as tall as he was, which he lowered down to point in front of him. They approached a lurking tiger with the confidence of those who were armed and thus had the upper hand. One man flushed out the striped beast with the flames and the other used the trident's points to poke and prod it in the Doctor's direction.

The Doctor didn't stay in one place, of course. The *bestiarii* were soon darting this way and that, trying to keep the animal on track. Although the Doctor was fairly confident he could keep this up all day, he suspected he wouldn't be allowed to do so. Better to get it over with. He stopped still and leaned casually against the marble wall.

'Come on, then!' he called to the approaching men, who grinned at the idea that they'd worn down their quarry at last.

'Having a good day?' the Doctor called up to the nearest seats, getting a cheer in response – except from the nearby Rufus, who scowled down at him. 'Hey, give us a smile!' the Doctor shouted to him. 'You should be happy – you've provided the crowd with the best show in ages, if I do say so myself.'

But Rufus kept scowling. And meanwhile the tiger was getting nearer, growling half at its tormentors and half at the Doctor.

The Doctor suddenly sprang into action, taking everyone by surprise, including the tiger. He dived over the beast's head, hands forward as if it were a vaulting horse. With a flip, he was standing at the creature's tail, arms in the air to mark a perfect landing. The torch-bearer was nearest and the Doctor grabbed the flaming brand from the shocked man, using it to knock the trident out of the other's grip. 'Don't try this at home, folks!' he yelled to the crowd, as the *bestiarii* stood stock still in stunned silence, unable to believe the way the tables had been turned. They remained like that for only a second, however. The Doctor was on the move again and they turned to follow.

But the tiger turned too. These men were the nearest – and they were the ones who had been taunting it, causing it pain…

The crowd was, temporarily, satisfied.

But the Doctor knew they'd soon be baying for his blood again. He could dodge and he could fight, but they would just keep sending more and more things at him, animals and men. He had to get out of there.

But no one had ever escaped from the arena.

NINE

Suddenly doors on the opposite side of the arena began to open. Someone had obviously decided on a change of tactics. Men were dragged through the doors, dozens of them forced at sword point. Voices called out to the Doctor and he recognised John, Paul, George and Ringo. Acquaintances of only a few hours, they seemed as close to him as brothers right now.

Stakes were standing around the arena and it was to these that the men were dragged, before having their arms lashed to the upright posts. The Doctor watched in horror as one *bestiarius* ran on with a heaped basket of raw meat, bits of which he flung at the feet of the bound men. There was no mistaking the message. The Doctor was putting up too much of a fight – the crowd needed guaranteed slaughter.

No sooner had the *bestiarii* retreated than the Doctor sped towards the men. Little Ringo was the closest and the Doctor freed him with a few slashes of the trident point. He handed the man the burning torch to protect himself, then ran off to the next stake. To his surprise – and delight – he saw Ringo heading over to another man. He used the torch to set light to the ropes – the flames obviously caused the man pain, but soon he was free.

The Doctor cut the ropes of the next prisoner. He pointed over to another stake, where Paul was tethered. 'Try to untie him,' the Doctor instructed.

Shaking, the man hurried off and began to comply.

The crowd screamed its disapproval. This wasn't what was supposed to happen.

More trapdoors opened. Half a dozen leopards leapt through. It took them a moment to get the scent, but then they were speeding towards the condemned men. The Doctor yelled for everyone to stand their ground, but a couple of the prisoners, too terrified to listen, made a bolt for it. The movement attracted the wild cats and once more the crowd had something to cheer about.

The remaining men gathered in a group, Ringo at the front frantically waving the torch to and fro. The group surged from one stake to another, the Doctor freeing each prisoner as others grabbed the chunks of raw meat, flinging them at the leopards to distract their attention.

The last man the Doctor reached was George. He was a rough-looking, dark-skinned man of about forty, but at the moment his face shone like an angel's. 'Is this really happening?' he said. 'Or have I died already?'

The Doctor grinned. 'Cooperation,' he said. 'Beautiful word. We're gonna make it out of here, you know.'

'I'm not asking for a miracle,' George told him.

'Just as well,' said the Doctor. 'Those who ask don't get, or so they say. But I reckon a miracle might just be on its way.'

The instant George was free, the Doctor raised a shout. 'To the wall!'

He led the group in a charge towards the arena's perimeter. A nearby door burst open and armed men appeared, the stumbling, sweaty forms of gaolers Flaccus and Thermus at the back. The prisoners, however, were too full of adrenalin to stop. The stunned guards suddenly found themselves falling beneath an onslaught of torch, trident, fists and just plain rage. By the time the fight was over, a number of the condemned men lay dead – but many others now wielded swords and stood over the bodies of their one-time captors.

Flaccus and Thermus had held back during the fight, waving their swords ineffectually. It was Paul who spotted them and alerted the others. The two guards backed away as the furious men turned on them.

'We were only following orders!' yelped Thermus.

'We did our best for you – don't you remember?' said Flaccus, gulping. 'Treated you like our own sons!'

'Treated us like scum, more like!' yelled Paul, brandishing a liberated sword in the air.

Flaccus and Thermus turned and fled.

And tripped right over the lion the Doctor had put to sleep earlier.

The lion woke up.

As the guards' screams died away, the Doctor's men made it to the wall at last. Those slain in the fight were acting as a diversion for the marauding beasts, but everyone was uncomfortably aware that their attention might be recaptured at any moment.

'What now?' gasped George, staring up at the marble wall. Even if they could climb it – which they couldn't – the fence on top of it would stop them going any further.

The Doctor looked up too. Not far above him he could see the furious face of Rufus, still cheated of the Doctor's blood. Next to Rufus, to the Doctor's absolute delight, he saw Gracilis, pulling at the magistrate's cloak. He grinned. The triumph of the little man, that's what all this was about.

He looked at the fence above him. Then he looked at the long trident he carried. Then he looked up again. He began to back away from the wall.

He grinned at his comrades. 'I've always fancied myself as an athlete,' he said. 'Now's the time to find out if the pole-vault's the event for me...'

He ran forward, plunging the trident into the ground and using it to launch himself into the air. The crowd gasped. No one could do this. He was going to impale himself on the fence spikes...

But he didn't. The Doctor let out a laugh of joy as he cleared the top and landed in a heap on top of two startled senators. 'Olympics, here I come!' Still laughing, he scrambled to his feet. 'Chuck us a sword,' he yelled down.

A blade came shooting into the air as George obliged. The Doctor caught it as it tumbled down his side of the fence.

'Now, we don't want any trouble,' he said, addressing the surrounding senators. 'And I don't want to hurt anyone. But I will if I have to. So it's in all your interests to do as I say. You,' he said, turning on the nearest man, 'give me your toga.'

The man hastily obliged, ripping off the purple-striped garment and handing it over.

'You too,' said the Doctor, and the next man also complied.

The Doctor tied the long strips of cloth together and

dangled the resulting rope over the side to Paul, who caught it and began to scale the arena's side.

Armed guards were beginning to appear in the stands, but the crowd was so thick they couldn't get close enough. Soon several prisoners armed with swords had crossed into the seating area and were holding everyone else at bay.

A shriek came from down below. The leopards had tired of their unmoving feast and were closing in on the living prey. Ringo was still waving his fire brand and George had the trident, but the cats seemed to regard their efforts as a challenge.

'Hold on,' called the Doctor, fumbling for his sonic screwdriver. 'I need to find another frequency…'

The Doctor's distraction nearly caused his death.

'Look out!' a voice suddenly cried. Gracilis!

The Doctor swung round. A dozen seats away, Gracilis was stumbling from a blow as Rufus raised a bow to fire. His fingers loosened on the string…

… and the Doctor raised the sonic screwdriver, spinning it like a tiny propeller. The arrow *zing*ed off and rattled harmlessly to the floor.

Rufus yelled in rage and sprang forward, trying for a better aim. A couple of the armed prisoners started forward towards him, but the Doctor yelled at them to stop – too many innocent people were in the way.

There was a cry from the stadium floor. A leopard had got through the defences and claimed a victim.

'Keep climbing!' the Doctor shouted urgently.

But that gave Rufus an idea. Grinning evilly, he leapt for the fence. Now his arrow pointed downwards – straight at John, who was halfway up the hanging togas. He moved to fire – but the shot never came. George's trident buried itself in the magistrate's chest and Rufus toppled into the arena. The leopard that had been about to spring on George turned its attention to this new delight.

The crowd were screaming and shrieking: horror, delight, fear.

Gracilis had got to his feet and was stumbling in the direction of the Doctor, but the milling multitudes wouldn't let him through.

'See you outside!' the Doctor called, gesturing for the old man to change course.

He turned back to the wall. Now George was climbing the rope. Ringo was last, flinging his torch at a prowling leopard as it darted towards him. As soon as Ringo's feet touched the floor, the Doctor was leading the way to the nearest exit. They weren't the only ones. Everyone nearby wanted to get out now, and that was still stopping the armed men from reaching the prisoners.

The Doctor waved a sword menacingly. 'Out! Out! Out!' he yelled.

Suddenly George was by his side. He looked shaken. 'I killed a magistrate,' he gasped. 'They were gonna kill me anyway – they'll show no mercy now.'

The Doctor gave him a reassuring smile. 'You saved a life,' he said simply. 'Now leg it – get out of here, get as far away as possible. Make good pies. And live.'

George gave him a nervous half-smile – and ran. As the Doctor watched him go, he reflected that he didn't even know the man's real name.

There was chaos on the streets outside. Luckily many of those outside had not been in the arena and were desperately trying to get details of what had happened from those who were leaving. The other lucky thing was that, because the arena was so enormous, few knew what the escaped men looked like close up.

The Doctor ducked and weaved through the crowds, throwing out an occasional 'How amazing was that?' to passers-by, or an, 'I've never seen anything like it!' Finally he spotted Gracilis among the masses and hurried towards him.

'Gracilis!'

The old man spun round eagerly. 'Doctor!'

They greeted each other warmly. Gracilis seemed almost in tears.

'I thought you were lost! First my son and then my friend. I have been trying to secure your release from your most unlawful punishment. I visited my contacts and tried to call in favours, but none will go against Rufus. So I followed the man to the arena, tried to reason with him, but he would not listen to me, and then – and then—'

The Doctor cut him off. 'Don't let's worry about that. It's all over now. Well, almost. Look, could you lend me your cloak?'

Unquestioningly, Gracilis unpinned his long cloak and handed it to the Doctor.

'Disguise,' the Doctor told him. Then he frowned. 'You'd better keep away from me. I mean, they don't know who I am and there's no record of my arrest, but that might not stop them tracking me down. I don't want you getting into trouble.'

The old man drew himself up to his full height. 'You have been helping me, Doctor, at great inconvenience to yourself. It is in many ways my fault that you are in this predicament at all. I will not desert a friend.'

'Thanks,' the Doctor said simply, but his warm smile said more.

They jogged along the street, trying to get as quickly as possible to the shrine of Fortuna, where the Doctor had been given the cure for Rose – and had heard the mysterious voice. They couldn't go as fast as he would have liked, for fear of attracting too much attention, but they made it at last, pushing their way through a crowd of schoolboys who were enjoying the holiday. The Doctor, realising he was still carrying a sword, handed it to a surprised youth, with instructions not to hurt anybody.

Finally they made it. The Doctor entered the temple at a run, shocking a young man who was preparing to present an offering.

'Hello?' the Doctor called, ignoring the man's presence. 'Anybody there?'

He went right up to the statue of Fortuna, standing in its alcove at the back. He peered behind it, but there was no one there. Whoever it had been, had he really expected them to hang around for a whole day?

'Hello?' he tried again, but with less conviction.

He turned away. One thing had gone – please let the other still be there. He retraced his steps from the day before. This was where he was standing when the armed men had grabbed him. This was where he'd been hit. This was where he'd dropped the phial…

There was no phial there. He dropped to his hands and knees, searching frantically.

'What is the matter, Doctor?' asked Gracilis, concerned.

'Someone – I mean, Fortuna gave me something she said would bring Rose back,' said the Doctor. 'And Optatus too.'

Gracilis's eyes shone. 'Do you mean this?' he asked, producing a glass phial of sparkling green liquid. 'Will this return my son to me?'

The Doctor jumped up, his face joyous. 'That's it!' he cried. 'Oh, thank you thank you thank you!' He took the phial and kissed it, and only just stopped himself from kissing Gracilis too.

'I found it on the floor here after your capture,' Gracilis explained, 'and I wondered if it might be something important.'

'I think it just might be,' said the Doctor. 'I mean, would Fortuna lie to me?'

He thought for a second, considering this seriously. It wasn't as if the circumstances were unsuspicious. But he had a definite feeling he could trust the strange voice. In fact, it had almost sounded familiar…

'Come on. First thing is to find a statue by Ursus.'

'Why?' asked Gracilis. 'If this potion can return my son to me…'

The Doctor wrinkled his nose. 'Just trust me,' he said. 'We're getting there. But we do need to find a statue first.'

The young man with the offering had been watching all of this in some bemusement and with perhaps not a little concern. Suddenly he cleared his throat.

'You are looking for a statue by the sculptor Ursus?' he asked nervously.

The Doctor spun round to face him. 'Too right we are. You know of one?'

The man nodded. 'I believe a new statue by Ursus is being unveiled in the forum today.'

The Doctor grinned. 'Yes! Gracilis, my old mate, it looks as if everything is coming up roses – no pun intended.'

He raised the phial. 'One miracle cure. One statue of Rose being unveiled. Rescue Rose, rescue Optatus, rescue everyone else, home in time for tea. Well, tomorrow's tea anyway. Or possibly breakfast the next day. Whatever, life is good!'

Still beaming, he led the way out of the shrine, and the two of them headed off towards the forum.

They entered by the magnificent Arch of Augustus, but the Doctor was in no mood to appreciate architecture. He scanned the hustle and bustle before him, the hundreds of people going about their daily business, meeting, shopping, orating – and the hundreds of statues, neither hustling nor bustling, that were watching them do it. Movement by a basilica, its walls already crowded with statues, caught his eye and he hurried over. A crowd had gathered there and he asked a woman what was happening.

'New statue,' she told him. 'By that bloke Ursus, the one everybody's talking about.'

The Doctor spared a second to thank her and then began to push his way through the masses, with Gracilis not far behind.

'Ladies and gentleman,' called a voice as the Doctor neared the front, 'I give you – the god Mercury!'

There was a cheer, but the Doctor did not join in. He could see the statue now. It was not Rose. It was the slave Tiro.

TEN

The Doctor's hearts sank as he gazed on the petrified Tiro. Gloomily, he called out to the man by the statue, 'Excuse me – isn't Ursus himself here to see his work take its place?'

The man shrugged. 'Nah. He's not even in Rome. We had to send a cart to fetch this from some country villa where he's staying.'

'He's not in Rome at all?' persisted the Doctor. 'You don't know of any other new statues of his that are being unveiled or anything? Something a bit more feminine perhaps. More Fortuna-y.'

'You can take my word for it,' said the man. 'Trust me, I'd know about it.'

'What do we do now?' asked Gracilis as the Doctor turned away. 'Back to the villa?'

The Doctor shook his head. 'No,' he said, 'there's work to do here first. Starting with this very statue. Don't want to cause a panic, so we'd better wait till nightfall...' He looked up at the sun, checking its position. 'Oh, who am I kidding? I can't wait that long. Let's start a panic. Oh – and let's hope this does what I think it does, or there might be a lynching instead!'

He turned back and hurried towards the statue, bounding onto a plinth to stand beside it. The people, who had begun to drift away, sensed there was more entertainment afoot and reversed their steps. If any of them recognised this sideburned showman as the arena escapee from earlier, however, they held their tongues – and as the citizens of Rome were not well known for their taciturnity or benevolence, chances were good that he hadn't been identified.

The Doctor took a bow, careful not to fall off the plinth. 'Ladies and gentlemen!' he cried, in imitation of the earlier announcement. 'I give you – the god Mercury!' No one seemed disposed to cheer at this repetition, so he carried on. 'As you know, this is a time of festivity. We have celebrated the divine Minerva, she of the shield and spear. Born fully grown and armoured out of the head of her father, believe it or not. Can't tell me that didn't hurt. Now we're carrying on the celebrations for the just as divine and even more warlike Mars. And d'you know what? They're really very grateful for your celebrations – not to mention your offerings and your getting very drunk in their names. And who better to bring their message of thanks to you than Mercury, messenger of the gods!'

The Doctor surreptitiously brought out the phial and carefully removed the stopper. He let a tiny drop of the jade-coloured liquid fall onto the marble of the statue.

'Ladies and gentlemen,' he said again, 'boys and girls, I give you Mercury!'

For a moment, the crowd looked on in bemusement. One or two turned away.

And then a woman screamed. And another.

Where there had been white marble, there was now a

blush of pink. It spread over the statue, the stone being eaten away by the stain of flesh. The painted lips became soft and pouting, the gilded eyes replaced by bright green orbs. Softly curled hair rippled and darkened and was caught by the breeze. Before the astonished crowd there now stood a living man, dressed in the winged hat and winged sandals of Mercury, holding up Mercury's *caduceus,* his staff with two snakes entwined around it. To even the Doctor's surprise, the stone snakes suddenly hissed, their scales turning yellow as they uncurled themselves from the staff and slithered away. That caused even more screaming from the crowd.

'Tell them you bring them a message of peace and love,' the Doctor hissed at the confused Tiro, grabbing him by the waist to stop him falling as he staggered forwards. 'Trust me. Then we can get out of here.'

Tiro, his bewildered eyes barely able to focus on the crowd in front of him, croaked out, 'I bring you a message of peace and love.'

The crowd went wild, shouting and screaming and cheering. The Doctor passed Tiro down to the stunned Gracilis, waiting below. 'Get him out of sight,' he whispered.

'Some entertainment for the festival!' the Doctor called, trying to regain the crowd's attention and allow Gracilis and Tiro to make their getaway. 'And here's a bit more!' He produced a small bronze coin. 'One *as*! Not worth much, but you wouldn't want to lose it.' He opened both his hands, palms flat. 'And I've only gone and lost it!' He pointed into the crowd. 'You, madam, have you seen my *as*? I beg your pardon, sir, I didn't quite catch that remark. You haven't? Then what, madam, is it doing in your ear?' He produced the coin seemingly from the lady's ear, to much delight.

'Me next! Me! Me!' called several children, who seemed more impressed with the Doctor's parlour trick than with the spectacle of a marble statue coming to life. The Doctor obliged for a while until he considered he'd given Gracilis and Tiro enough time, then made his own escape, leaving behind a number of delighted children who were considering how to spend their bounty.

He found the others lurking discreetly behind a pillar in a quiet street. Both looked rather shaken.

'If I had not seen it with my own eyes...' Gracilis muttered.

'Bit of a shock for you both,' said the Doctor. 'Might have made it easier if I'd explained earlier that Ursus is an... evil sorcerer who's been going around turning people to stone for his own ends. There again, might not've. Anyway, we've got work to do.'

He strode off again, leaving the stunned pair to follow in his wake.

'You mean,' said Gracilis, jogging to catch him up, 'that Optatus...'

The full horror of the situation suddenly seemed to hit him and he would have fallen to the floor if Tiro hadn't been on hand to catch him.

The Doctor stopped. 'Yes,' he said. 'I think you've got the idea. I'm very sorry. But we're going to bring him back, just as soon as we've done all the rest.'

The remainder of the day was spent scouring Rome for all Ursus's statues. Gracilis, as an art lover, knew the right people to talk to, so he was able not only to discover all the locations but also to ascertain that, as far as anyone knew, the sculptor's statues were exhibited only in Rome itself. Other than Gracilis's, no one knew of any private commissions outside the city walls.

One by one, the statues were restored to their living states. Diana became a beautiful black woman holding a bow. The Doctor handed over Gracilis's cloak to an embarrassed Venus. Twins Castor and Pollux hugged each other then the Doctor in delight and relief. Bewildered slave after bewildered slave stepped off their plinths, to be told that they had 'been under a spell'. To the Doctor's relief, this inadequate explanation seemed to satisfy them.

'But who are all these people?' Gracilis asked at one point.

'I imagine,' said the Doctor, 'that they're slaves bought by Ursus for this particular purpose.'

Gracilis frowned. 'Then they still belong to Ursus,' he said. 'We have no right to take them away.'

The Doctor fixed Gracilis with a very hard stare. 'True,' he said. 'In Roman law, a master may treat his slave how he likes. He can flog him, torture him, kill him, turn him into a novelty marble doorstop if he thinks it's a good idea. And you're a good Roman, I know that. But look me in the eye and tell me you think what Ursus has done here is OK.'

Gracilis broke eye contact.

'I think Rome may become a bit too hot for Ursus in the near future,' continued the Doctor. 'Not counting what might happen when I catch up with him. I am, it's true, known for my forgiving nature, but even so...' He raised a hand to stop Gracilis speaking. 'I don't want to hear what should happen to these slaves. I only want to hear what will happen. I think you're a good man. So I think what's going to happen is you're going to make sure they're all all right.'

Beaten, Gracilis nodded.

The Doctor slapped him on the back. 'Good man!'

Soon there was only a tiny amount of the glistening green potion left, and the Doctor guarded it as though it was the most precious thing in the universe. Right at the moment, it was.

'I never thought I should see such magic,' said Gracilis in awe, as the Doctor replaced the stopper once again, and sent Juno – and her bewildered peacock – to wait by Gracilis's carriage outside the city gates, where the other slaves were congregating.

'Not magic,' said the Doctor, more to himself than to the old man. 'Science.' But he didn't admit, even to himself, that he had no idea how science had created the miraculous liquid – or where it had come from.

As they roamed through the streets they heard talk of festival tricks, of magic, of gods walking in the world of men. The Doctor grinned at the words, but Gracilis grew more and more nervous, convinced they would be arrested at any moment – but determined to carry on to the bitter end.

'What are they going to do to us?' said the Doctor, trying to reassure him. 'Unless it's Opposite Day, they can't charge us with bringing people back to life.'

Finally there was just one statue to go, and, according to Gracilis's contacts, it was to be found in a grove of trees near the Theatre of Pompey. But there was a shock in store as they arrived. The grove was entirely surrounded by armed guards.

The Doctor sauntered over. 'What's going on?' he said, innocent curiosity shining from his face.

'Someone has been nicking all the statues by the sculptor

Ursus,' a guard told him. 'But they're not getting this one. See them getting it past us!'

The Doctor tutted. 'What is the world coming to?'

He was thinking hard as he wandered casually back to Gracilis. Only one statue to go, compared to the dozens already liberated. If they risked this and got into trouble, what would that mean for Rose and Optatus?

But through the trees he'd spotted the gleam of marble. The statue of a young girl standing on a pedestal. A girl of about Rose's age, her whole life ahead of her.

So of course he couldn't leave.

'How are you going to get past all those men?' Gracilis asked, worried.

The Doctor thought for a moment. Then his face lit up. 'Getting in isn't the problem,' he said. 'What they're worried about is someone getting out with the statue. Well – I wasn't planning on doing that! Now, I just need you to engage a couple of them in conversation, distract them while I slip in...'

The Doctor crept into the grove. Most of the guards were around the perimeter, but there was one actually standing by the statue itself. Luckily he had his back to it, but even so...

Carefully, quietly, the Doctor padded closer. The statue was that of an Earth goddess, a buxom young woman who radiated comfort and solicitude even in stone form. The Doctor drew the stopper from the phial, then reached up to place a hand over her marble mouth. A single drop and she was whole again, a human being. The panic rose in her eyes as the Doctor swung her down from her plinth, but something in his expression must have reassured her. He put a finger to his lips as he took her hand, and they stumbled off into the trees together.

'Hiya, Gaia,' the Doctor whispered to the one-time Earth goddess as they crouched behind a tree trunk. 'Don't worry. Everything's going to be all right.' He had trouble not laughing as they watched the armed man still blithely guarding the empty stone pedestal. 'Just follow my lead.'

'Oi!' called a guard as the Doctor and the girl walked out of the trees and made to cross the armed line.

The Doctor beamed at him. 'Hello.'

'No one's allowed in there!'

'We're not in there,' the Doctor pointed out, reasonably. 'We're out here.'

'What were you doing in there? We searched it all.'

'Well,' said the Doctor, 'you obviously missed us. Not hard to do. No blame attached to you, I'm sure. My, er, friend and I –' The guard sniggered knowingly – 'must have fallen asleep in the afternoon sun. Still, we're wide awake now, so if you'd just let us leave…'

'Hey!' The shout came from inside the grove. 'The statue's gone!'

The Doctor was suddenly surrounded by guards. He put on his best blasé expression.

'Where is it?' demanded a guard.

'Where's what?' asked the Doctor.

'The statue! You must have taken it – no one's been allowed inside!'

The Doctor raised his arms. 'Please, search me,' he said. 'If you think I have a statue concealed in my tunic somewhere…'

'Then you've got it out already.'

'What, I just walked past all you armed gentlemen with a bloomin' great statue – and then returned for the fun of it?'

The guards looked at each other, floored but reluctant to give up on their one hope of avoiding ignominious failure. Suddenly the man who'd been guarding the sculpture spoke up. ''Ere,' he said, pointing at the Doctor's companion, 'she don't 'alf look like that statue. Even those clothes what she's wearing.'

The Doctor slapped his palm against his forehead. 'Of course! That's it! You've got me bang to rights. What I actually did was sneak in there, transform the statue into this young lady and then try to casually walk out with her. What a fool I was to think I could get away with it with you fine gentlemen on guard. I'll just come quietly, shall I?'

At that moment, Gracilis wandered up to them. 'Is there a problem, Doctor?' he said. 'I am Gnaeus Fabius Gracilis,' he told the guards importantly, 'and this man is my friend. May I inquire as to why you are detaining him?'

Grumbling and suspicious, the guards let the Doctor and 'Gaia' pass.

'Thanks,' said the Doctor, thumping Gracilis on the back. 'Told you we could do it. Now – let's get out of here...'

Gracilis arranged transport for the slaves, and then he and the Doctor headed for his own carriage.

'Back to my son, at last!' Gracilis cried, beaming.

The Doctor was less happy. He had every confidence in his ability to track down Rose, but that didn't change the fact that, right at this moment, he had no idea where she was. A thought suddenly struck him.

'And we can check up on Vanessa too,' he said. 'There's been no word from her, has there? I hope she's OK.'

But at the moment all Gracilis could think of was that he had a son to save.

As they walked towards the city gates, the Doctor spotted a familiar-looking street. 'Hold on a tick,' he said. 'I don't suppose there's room in that excellent carriage of yours for a rather stylish blue box?'

It was late afternoon the next day. The carriage carrying the Doctor and Gracilis approached the villa, closely followed by a hired cart bearing the solid blue shape of the TARDIS. (The Doctor had been right – there hadn't been room in the carriage.) Gracilis ordered the carriage to stop before they reached the villa itself. 'I want to bring Optatus to my wife,' he said. 'I do not want her to witness his restoration. I fear the knowledge of what truly happened would disturb her mind.'

They walked to the grove and Gracilis stared at the statue, not speaking. Perhaps, now the moment had come, he was too scared to rush in, knowing that his hopes could still be dashed. But finally he nodded to the Doctor.

The Doctor stepped forward and let one of the last remaining precious drops of green liquid fall on the stone.

Even the Doctor didn't breathe as they waited, microseconds feeling like hours.

Then it happened. The spread of flesh, the blinking of an eye, an arm slumping down from its noble pose.

And then Optatus was in his father's arms and both were weeping.

The Doctor looked on from a distance as Optatus was reunited with his mother. Her tears flowed freely, but she couldn't stop smiling. Finally, after it seemed that everyone had calmed down, he approached. He couldn't stop Marcia from bursting into tears again, hugging him and thanking him so many times that the words began to sound in his ears like a nonsense chant, but eventually he was able to ask her his questions. Had she seen Rose? Or Ursus? Had there been any word from Vanessa?

The answer to all his questions was 'no'.

The Doctor slid away from the celebrations. Hopelessness was not a feeling he would ever admit to, but right now the Roman world stood before him impossibly large and discouraging. Rose was a tiny marble needle in a giant Roman haystack. How would he ever find her?

And then he had a thought. A real humdinger of a thought, a blast-between-the-eyes thought.

He knew exactly where he could find Rose.

ELEVEN

The bright blue of the TARDIS screamed incongruity amid the clinical white walls and anaemic marble of the sculpture room. However, the Doctor, still dressed in his Roman tunic, blended in with the exhibits in a way no other visitor did – yet he was the one who got strange looks from the camera-laden tourists in sloganed T-shirts and the dusty academics wearing tweed jackets.

As far as the Doctor was concerned, though, these people didn't exist – even the kids prodding at the TARDIS, assuming it to be some sort of interactive display, got barely a glance. He was a man on a mission and he was not going to be distracted.

But when he reached Rose's statue, something distracted him.

Perched on the big toe of the nearby giant foot – in blatant disregard of the signs forbidding anyone to touch the exhibits – was a familiar figure. Mickey Smith.

'Doctor!' Mickey said as the Doctor approached. He looked over the Doctor's shoulder – but the Doctor was alone. 'Oh. Wotcha.'

The Doctor slowed his frantic pace. 'Hello,' he replied.

'So... is this before or after the last time?'

Mickey shrugged. 'How do I know what the last time is for you? Last time for me was a fortnight ago, when you and Rose went off to make her the toast of the art world.'

The Doctor winced.

'And I guess you got there all right,' Mickey continued, looking the Doctor up and down, 'or are man-skirts in this season?'

The Doctor ignored him, concentrating on the statue before him.

Rose's youthful beauty captured for ever. Even petrified, the strength shone out of her face. No one could look at this and not realise what a special person she was. He unconsciously reached out a hand to hold hers. But of course, it wasn't there.

Suddenly, a wave of doubt threatened to overcome him.

Mickey had got up and was standing beside him. 'You know, whoever made this must have really known her,' he said. 'It's like... like they really understood her.' He paused, then had a sudden thought. 'Hey, she wasn't, you know, seeing this fella or anything, was she?'

The Doctor laughed harshly – inhumanly – and Mickey took a step back. 'Whoa! Didn't mean to step on your toes, man.'

'This isn't a statue of Rose,' the Doctor said.

Mickey looked confused. 'What're you talking about? Course it is. Think I don't know Rose when I see her?'

'No, you don't,' said the Doctor. 'Because you're looking at her right now. This isn't a statue of Rose. This is Rose herself. Rose has been turned into stone.'

Mickey had sat back down on the foot and was cradling his

head in his hands. 'It's not true,' he was saying, the words high and muffled, his body heaving with the sobs that he was trying to suppress, trying to hide.

A uniformed official approached them. 'Excuse me, sir,' he said to Mickey, seemingly oblivious of the tears. 'I'm afraid I must ask you not to sit on the exhibits.'

Mickey ignored him; probably didn't even hear him.

'He's a bit upset right now,' the Doctor pointed out.

The man was unmoved. 'I'm sorry, sir, but I cannot make an exception.'

The Doctor stepped closer and prodded him. 'Sorry, just checking if you were really human. Because a real human would see just how upset my… friend is and show a bit of compassion.'

The guard ignored the Doctor's anger. Probably used to that sort of thing, even in as refined a place as a museum. He spoke so reasonably that the Doctor, not in the best of moods just at the moment, felt his ire rise even higher. 'We have a duty to protect these items. They wouldn't have lasted for countless generations if everyone had been allowed to go around sitting on them, would they?'

The Doctor was about to launch into a number of counter-arguments involving past uses of stone works – as well as uses that had just come to him and in which the guard could possibly take part – all of which would probably have had the man doubting his sanity, when Mickey pushed himself to his feet. He shoved his face towards that of the security guard.

'I don't care about your stupid statues or your stupid duty!' he shouted.

Everyone else in the room turned to stare. One tourist took a photo.

'She's dead! Don't you understand? She's dead! I've been coming here every day, every single stupid day, just to feel I was close to her – to keep me going until I saw her again. But I didn't know… now I'm not going to see her again, not ever!'

'I'm sorry, sir, but—'

The Doctor stepped in before the situation got any worse. 'As I told you, he's a bit upset right now,' he said harshly, and took Mickey by the arm.

Silent tears still coursed down Mickey's cheeks as the Doctor led him out of the room and up the stairs; he looked dazed and angry.

The Doctor sat him down at a table in the Great Court and went off to a nearby counter. He returned with two plastic cups of blackcurrant cordial and placed one in front of Mickey, sticking a straw in the top.

They sat silently for a few minutes. Neither one of them was really there any more; they were in the past, with Rose. Talking to her. Laughing with her. Just looking at her face.

'She was always too good for me,' Mickey said suddenly. 'Didn't deserve her, I didn't. There was this time I had the flu – she looked after me, every day. I felt like I wanted to die, then she'd hold my hand and I'd remember how good life could be.' He almost smiled. 'I thought I was the luckiest man alive to get her. We were only kids, but I knew she was special. Kept thinking she'd leave me. And she did, once. Came back, though. Thought she was on the rebound, that she'd see sense after a week or two. But she didn't. Never thought I'd hang on to her a second time. Knew there was something better out there and she'd realise it in the end. I just had to make the most of every day I got. I mean, I was angry when she went off with you. Angry with you, but angry with her too, angry that she'd seen through me at last. Realised I was a loser and she was a winner. But I didn't mind, not in the end. Because she deserved more than me. She deserved someone who could give her the whole universe.' The sorrow in his voice turned to anger. 'But you got her killed.'

'I know,' said the Doctor, and it was as if he hated himself.

'You got her killed and I'll never see her again! She thought she wanted danger and excitement – but you could have stopped her! She wasn't a – a *Time Lord*, she was just an ordinary girl and you got her killed.'

'Rose wasn't "ordinary",' said the Doctor. He stopped sounding angry at himself, directed it at Mickey instead. 'What was I supposed to do? Wrap her in cotton wool? Tell her, "Here, I could give you the universe, but I'm not going to in case you get hurt? There's all this stuff out there, all these planets, all these wonders, but I want you to stay at home and work in a shop?"'

Mickey stood up and yelled, 'You should have taken better care of her!'

The Doctor shouted back, 'I know!'

Mickey sat back down. 'You should've,' he repeated quietly. He suddenly shivered. 'How'm I gonna tell her mum? She'll crucify me.'

'I think you mean me,' said the Doctor. He gave a half-laugh. 'Funnily enough, I was almost crucified this morning. Luckily, they threw me to the lions instead.'

Mickey concentrated on the first bit, too wrapped up in what was happening right now to care in the slightest about the Doctor's adventures. 'Like you'll stick around. And Jackie'll have to take it out on someone. She ain't got anyone else any more.' His face crumpled. 'She won't even have a grave!'

The Doctor was quiet for a few minutes, letting Mickey's tears run their course. Then he said, almost hesitantly, 'I can bring her back.'

Mickey looked up, astonished. 'You what?'

The Doctor spoke again, more assured this time. 'I can bring her back.'

Mickey jumped to his feet, almost more angry than before. 'You… you can? Well, why didn't you say so before? Was this fun for you, seeing me like this? Mickey the idiot, doesn't understand this stuff, let's have a laugh with him?' He looked as though he was about to punch the Doctor, who stepped in quickly.

'I… wasn't sure if it was the right thing to do.' He waved a hand, silencing Mickey's next protest. 'But now I am. So isn't the fact that I can do it the most important thing here?'

Mickey seemed about to argue – but then he nodded. 'Yeah. Right. Well, what are we waiting for, then?' He started walking.

'For that guard to go away for a start,' the Doctor called after him.

Mickey stumped back and sat down again.

They were both silent for a few moments. The Doctor took a long swig of blackcurrant cordial.

Then Mickey said, a bit nervously, 'But… won't she be, like, 2,000 years old or something?'

'Closer to 1,900, give or take the odd change of calendar,' the Doctor replied. 'That shouldn't… that *won't* matter. She's not aware in there. She hasn't aged.'

'Are you sure she's not aware?' asked Mickey. 'Are you sure she hasn't been watching everything that's going on?'

The Doctor raised an eyebrow. 'Well, if she has, she'll

have seen you every day for the last fortnight. That should earn you Brownie points.' He'd meant it almost – almost – kindly, but Mickey looked like a puppy that had been kicked. He sighed. 'Come on,' he said, standing up. 'Let's see if the coast is clear.'

But Mickey remained seated. 'Rose might not have aged – not the Rose inside. But that statue has. It's got chips out of it. Its hand's got knocked off. Will that come back when you bring her to life again?'

The Doctor didn't answer.

'It won't, will it?' Mickey said, furious. 'It won't grow back magically like yours did. You're going to bring her back with chips off and a hand missing!'

The Doctor thumped the table. 'It's better than no Rose at all!' he shouted.

Mickey looked a bit scared. But after a few seconds, he nodded. 'Yeah,' he said. 'I guess it is.'

As they made their way back to the sculpture room, the Doctor heard Mickey mutter, 'I just hope she agrees.'

It was the end of the day and people were beginning to drift out of the museum. There were a couple of tourists wandering past the rows of stone heads in the sculpture room, but no one else was near Rose.

The Doctor held up the small phial with its few drops of precious, life-giving liquid. Hand steady, he took a deep breath. And then his hand turned and the potion poured onto the statue.

Nothing happened.

No blush of flesh to the cheeks. No ripple of cloth or flutter of eyelashes.

The Doctor just stared.

'How long's it take to work, then?' Mickey asked.

'It's not going to work,' said the Doctor dully. 'It's too late. She must have been stone too long.' He paused. 'It's over.'

Mickey wouldn't accept it. 'That's rubbish. You've got a time machine. Oh, I know all that laws of time stuff, you can't stop it happening, but you can find her earlier. Change her back then.'

The Doctor shook his head, frustrated and angry. 'Don't you see? If I changed her back then, then this –' he gestured at the statue – 'wouldn't be here now! That's why I couldn't find her back in Rome. I was never meant to find her! There's nothing I can do!' He flung out his arm, hand brushing against Rose's face.

He looked again at the statue.

And he went mad.

Mickey watched in alarm as the Doctor ran to the TARDIS, yelling 'Oh, please! Oh, please!' at the top of his voice. A moment later he emerged from the ship, carrying Rose's denim jacket.

The Doctor held it up and shook it.

Out fell a purse, a hankie, a packet of mints, a mobile phone and an earring.

He retrieved the earring and held it up to the statue.

'It's the same one,' said Mickey.

'She forgot to put it back on,' said the Doctor. 'So Rose – the real Rose – is only wearing one earring. But the statue has two. That means this...' He let it sink in. 'This isn't Rose. This is just – a statue.' He pulled himself together. 'I've got to go back and find her.' He stared at the glass phial. There was the tiniest hint of liquid still in the bottom. 'This had better be enough...'

Mickey's face was shining with relief. But a thought struck him. 'Hang on, though. How did this statue get to be here, then?'

The Doctor grinned. 'I've got an idea about that. Do you believe in gods?'

Mickey looked bewildered. 'No.'

'Well, right at this moment I do,' said the Doctor. 'I think Fortuna here is smiling on us. Come on. I need you to give me a hand here...'

They'd just finished when the security guard came rushing back in.

'Time for a quick getaway, I think,' said the Doctor. He pushed Mickey towards the stairs and then dashed for the TARDIS.

'You will get her back, won't you?' Mickey yelled.

'You can bet on it!' cried the Doctor. But as he shut the TARDIS doors behind him, he muttered to himself, 'I've just got to make a quick stop on the way...'

And then, some time later, the Doctor arrived in Rome some time earlier.

TWELVE

Rose gasped, as if someone had thrown a bucket of cold water over her. She spluttered awake, dazed and confused.

She had shut her eyes for a second and when she opened them again she was in a completely different place. This wasn't Ursus's workshop; this was... leaves. She could see leaves. Branches. Trees. This was a wood. And she was standing next to something with wheels... Car? No. Penny-farthing bicycle? No. A wooden cart! And there in front of her, something tall, thin – a person – definitely not Ursus. A great big grin swam into focus. The Doctor!

She stumbled forward and enveloped him in a huge hug. 'Boy, am I pleased to see you!'

He yelped. 'Ow!'

She'd forgotten she was holding a spear. 'Sorry,' she said, grinning. She took off the uncomfortable helmet and shook her head to clear it.

He raised an eyebrow. 'Rose Tyler, warrior queen?'

'Yeah,' she said. 'I'm planning on popping home and rampaging through Colchester.'

'Ah, I know you wouldn't say "Boo-dicca" to a goose,' the Doctor replied, and she groaned.

'Yeah, but, look, how's this work?' she said. 'Last thing I remember…' She fell silent.

The Doctor looked a bit sheepish. 'You got turned into stone,' he said. 'Sorry.'

The memories flooded back. 'I knew,' she said. 'When he showed me the statue of Tiro, I knew.' She shivered.

The Doctor smiled sadly, sympathetically. 'Don't think about it any more. And Tiro's going to be OK. I'm going to rescue him, in, ooh, a day or two.'

Rose wrinkled her brow and he explained.

'That's the beauty of time travel. I've arrived back a few days before I left.' He handed her the now-empty phial. 'There you go. One miracle restorative. Roll up, roll up! Does your head feel like it's full of rocks? A drop of our potion will sort you out. Ladies, does your husband receive all your loving comments in stony silence? Give him our amazing remedy and he'll be a new man in no time at all.'

Rose grinned. 'So where did that come from, then? And where's Ursus? Did you sort him out?'

'Don't really know. Somewhere around and not yet.'

'You're lost without me!'

He tucked his arm through hers. 'Don't I just know it? If anyone ever asks me what sort of friend you are, I tell them: Rose Tyler? I'm lost without her. Rock-solid, that's what she is.'

Rose growled at him, but it turned into a laugh halfway through. 'There's another thing I don't understand, though,' she said when she'd stopped laughing. 'How's this all fit in with that statue in the British Museum? I mean, look at me!'

The Doctor did so. 'Helmet, spear, oh-so-noble profile – Minerva, unless I'm very much mistaken,' he said. 'Tell you what, though, that outfit'd go down great at parties. Or you could be a Minerva-gram. Any red-blooded – or blue-blooded, or green-blooded – male would love a Minerva-gram. And the great thing is, if any of them get out of hand, there you are with a weapon handy!'

Rose stopped him. 'Yeah, but who is Minerva?'

'Who indeed? Some say –' The Doctor caught Rose's stern eye and decided to cut out the more elaborate explanation. 'Goddess of war and the arts, patron of artisans.'

'"War and the arts"?' said Rose. 'What, like, "Say you like my painting or I'll invade your country"? Anyway, my point was, what happened to all that Fortuna stuff?'

'Well—' began the Doctor.

He didn't get a chance to explain. There was a sudden cry from behind them. Rose made to run, but the Doctor held her back. 'It's all right,' he said. 'It's only Vanessa.'

The girl was walking towards them, a look of total shock on her face. She was staring at the Doctor as if he were a ghost.

'How... how did you get here?' she said. 'You can't possibly have got here before me.'

'You of all people should know that anything's possible,' said the Doctor. 'Rose,' he continued, turning to her, 'let me reintroduce you to Vanessa, who is not an astrologer or a Roman slave, but a girl from the year 2375.'

'Blimey,' said Rose. 'And I thought I was a long way from home.' She turned to Vanessa. 'What you doing here, then?'

'Trying to get home,' said Vanessa.

'But how d'you get here in the first place?' asked Rose.

'Yes, I'd be interested to know that too,' said the Doctor. 'But Vanessa keeps avoiding the question. She seems to have something to hide.'

Vanessa looked as if she was about to burst into tears. 'I don't! I just… you just wouldn't believe me. You really wouldn't.'

'Go on, try us,' said Rose. 'Can it really be any worse than us going around thinking you're connected with what's going on here?'

Vanessa flushed. 'But… I think I might be.'

Rose took a step back. 'I've been telling everyone you're one of the good guys!'

'But I am! It's just… Oh, all right, I'll tell you everything!' cried Vanessa miserably.

She flung herself down by a tree. Rose and the Doctor sat nearby.

'I am Vanessa Moretti, gamma daughter of Salvatorio Moretti of the Bureau Tygon.'

'Suddenly it all becomes clear,' said the Doctor flippantly.

Rose *shh*ed him.

'The Bureau Tygon is the main scientific research establishment,' Vanessa continued.

Now the Doctor's ears really did prick up. 'And your father was working on time travel?' he said. 'Now why have I never heard—'

'No!' Vanessa interrupted his interruption. 'He worked in AI.'

'What, the film with that boy from *The Sixth Sense* in?' said Rose.

'Artificial intelligence,' the Doctor told her.

'Yeah, I know,' she said, and gestured for Vanessa to continue.

'He never mentioned anything to do with time travel. I mean, it's not possible, everyone knows that.' She smiled sadly, correcting herself. 'Everyone thought they knew that.

My father was working on some project – an AI project. He wasn't very enthusiastic to start with, said it was just a toy, a money-maker. But he began to get more excited. I think it was close to completion when I… left.

'He'd brought something home to work on that day – I don't know what. But then he got called out. I'd been watching a vidcast on ancient Rome.' She laughed ruefully. 'I used to love history. But my caster packed up. I thought something was wrong with the power supply because the lights kept flickering, but I went down to see if the caster in my father's study was still working and it was. There was a box on the side and I think it must have held whatever it was he was working on, but I didn't look to see.

'Anyway, I sat down to watch the cast. It was about the reign of Hadrian. About building the Pantheon and the wall and everything. Then I got a telecall from my friend Ariane. I was telling her what I was watching, and I said – I remember this, because it was the last thing I said – that I wished I lived back then.' She began to laugh hysterically. 'Can you believe that? Can you believe I said that? Live in a time like this! I must have been mad!'

Rose reached out and took her hand, trying to calm her down. 'Yeah, well, things never turn out how you imagine them, do they? It's what keeps divorce lawyers in business.'

'And what happened then?' asked the Doctor, more concerned about Vanessa's story than her feelings.

Vanessa swallowed her hysteria with a few hiccups. After a couple of goes, she managed to continue. 'Then… Then the call went dead. The caster shut down. The lights went off. I felt like I was about to be sick… and then I was here.'

The Doctor wasn't satisfied. 'There has to be more to it than that.'

'Well, there isn't!' Vanessa insisted. 'I didn't have a clue what had happened. I thought… I thought I must be dreaming. Or hallucinating. Or someone was playing some elaborate trick on me. But after a few weeks I pretty much gave up on that idea.'

'And you still don't know how you got here?' said Rose.

Vanessa shook her head.

'So why do you think you might have something to do with what Ursus is up to?'

'There's no such thing as time travel and yet here I am, thousands of years before my birth. It's impossible to turn people to stone and yet it's happening here. Two impossibles…'

'… don't necessarily make a possible,' the Doctor completed. 'And anyway, time travel is perfectly possible, if far too advanced for your society.'

Rose shrugged apologetically at Vanessa. 'But turning people to stone…' she said.

'Isn't impossible either. We're talking something extremely complex at a molecular level – not something that your average ancient Roman could have managed, true, but not impossible.'

'So, not magic, then,' said Rose.

'Don't be silly, Rose,' said the Doctor.

'Or petrifold regression?'

He raised an eyebrow. 'My, you have been paying attention. Nope, that takes weeks.'

'So… is Ursus from the twenty-fourth century too?'

The Doctor shook his head. 'Gracilis has known him since he was a child.' He suddenly jumped up. 'Ursus! Where is he?'

Rose shrugged. 'How should I know?'

'He brought you here...'

'Well, I wasn't really paying attention at the time,' said Rose. 'I was a bit too busy standing very still and having pigeons pooing on me.'

The Doctor waved for her to be quiet. 'Yes, yes, I know... But he wouldn't have brought you here for no reason, just left you... And I was right behind, so I'd have seen him if he went back towards the road...' He was pacing about now, examining the ground. 'Footprints!' he cried after a moment. 'Come on!'

Rose scrambled to follow him as he set off, with Vanessa on her heels.

'Couldn't get the cart any further, that's why he left you here,' the Doctor said after a while.

'You don't say,' said Rose. 'What do you think stopped him?'

They were weaving between trees, picking their way along paths that were barely there – or not there at all. She tried to clear the path with her spear, but brambles still tore harshly at her skin and clothes. The Doctor, spearless, still somehow managed to avoid them all.

'I'm really not dressed for this,' Rose muttered, thinking longingly of jeans and sturdy boots. 'Ow!' she exclaimed, as a branch stuck in her once-elaborately styled hair. She wished she'd kept Minerva's helmet on. 'Still, on the plus side, no one's going to ask me to do any modelling looking like this. Or be a Minerva-gram either.'

The Doctor carried on with his own train of thought. 'He was probably planning to come back for you.'

'If he could find his way back,' said Rose. 'Because I'm not sure I'm going to be able to.' They seemed to have been following the trail for miles, even though they probably hadn't been, and as far as she could see all the trees looked pretty much alike.

'But where was he going?' asked Vanessa.

The Doctor – who didn't seem to have so much as a hair out of place – came to a halt. 'There, I think.'

Rose peeked round a tree. There was a clearing in front of them, only a small one, but enough for there to be a break in the tree-top canopy overhead. Rose hadn't realised how dark it had been among the trees until the sunlight hit her and dazzled her eyes. As they came back into focus, she realised what the Doctor had been talking about. In the clearing was a small stone building, a derelict husk with gaping holes in its walls.

'What is it?' she whispered. 'Some sort of shrine?'

The Doctor nodded. 'I think so,' he said. 'A very old one. Abandoned, obviously – well, by most people. You know, tomorrow is the Quinquatrus. I think Ursus is planning to hold his very own festival here.'

There was a noise from inside the shrine: a scuffling sound.

'Maybe not that abandoned,' said Rose.

They crept forward, silent as mice, and peered through a gap in the nearest wall. Rose and Vanessa both had to stifle gasps as the Doctor frowned at them to be quiet.

Ursus was inside – but so was a woman. She was turned away, so they couldn't see her properly, but Rose could tell she was clearly wearing a helmet and carrying a shield and spear. She reminded her of the picture of Britannia on the back of a fifty-pence piece, but something more than that... Ursus had dressed Rose herself in a helmet like that, made her carry a spear like that. That meant this woman too was dressed as the goddess Minerva. Rose grimaced –

he obviously had some sort of art/war goddess thing going on, and she felt unclean at the thought she'd been a part of it.

But then the woman turned and this time Rose wasn't able to stop herself gasping. The light! The light that shone from the woman's eyes! The beautiful, ethereal glow from her face! The way her hair swam out around her head in a halo, as though she were under water.

This woman wasn't dressed as the goddess Minerva.

She was the goddess Minerva.

Ursus was speaking. 'I have created the most perfect work to honour you, at this time of your festival,' he said.

The Doctor nudged Rose. 'That's you!' he whispered, rather insensitively she thought.

She nudged him back and kept listening.

Minerva nodded. 'And you will be rewarded for your devotion,' she said, in a voice like honey and rose petals. 'As long as you make offerings to me, I will give you what you desire.'

'I don't think I want to watch this…' murmured Rose.

There was another sound from the temple, a frightened *baaa*. Ursus was carrying forward a baby lamb.

'I really don't want to watch this!' said Rose, as the sculptor held up a knife. 'Oi! You! Stop!' She was halfway into the shrine before the Doctor could react. No cute farmyard animals were being slaughtered on her watch…

The knife hung in the air as she charged forward. It dropped, lower, lower… Rose felt as if she was in slow motion.

She was in slow motion. The goddess was looking at her with those unearthly, shining eyes, and she wasn't able to run any more.

She was dimly aware of the Doctor and Vanessa following her into the temple.

She was dimly aware of the painful, heartbreaking final bleat of the lamb as its lifeblood ran onto the floor, and of Ursus's triumphant cry.

But all she could see was the goddess, blood pooling around her feet.

And then – horribly – the blood began to vanish, as if the goddess was a sponge, soaking it up. Then the body of the lamb, already tiny, began to shrink. Its essence was liquefying, puddling where the blood had been and being sucked up in its turn until there was not a woolly fragment left.

THIRTEEN

Rose stared at where the lamb had once been. She felt sick.

'Don't be upset, Rose,' Minerva said. 'Even gods must eat. It is no different from you consuming –' she paused, as if searching for the right words – 'a lamb chop or a kebab.'

'Right,' said Rose, dazed. 'Er, I think maybe I won't be doing that any more.'

'Come forward, Doctor, Vanessa,' the goddess continued. 'No harm will befall you here.'

'Are you sure?' said the Doctor. 'Because your follower Ursus there has been going around doing quite a lot of harm actually.'

Ursus stepped forward. 'Watch your tongue when you speak to the goddess!' he snarled.

The Doctor frowned. 'I think that would make speaking rather difficult,' he said. He stuck his tongue out and crossed his eyes to look down on it. 'Therterly inghockigal,' he said.

Ursus growled, and the Doctor shrugged and spoke normally. 'Are you denying you've been doing harm, then? Because I really think you have been. You know, with all that turning people to stone and so on. Call me a philistine if you like – although actually the Philistines weren't as bad as all that. They might not know a good painting if they saw one, but they knew how to throw a classy party... Where was I? Oh, yes – call me a philistine, but I can't quite see the justification of the petrification-as-art business.'

'Art justifies everything,' Ursus said simply.

'Er, no, it doesn't,' the Doctor replied. 'One nil to me. Next?'

'Without art, life would have no meaning!'

'Hmm. Actually don't entirely disagree with you on that one, believe it or not – but, and I think this may be the point at which we part company, there's already quite a lot of art in the world. Mosaics, paintings, music – even rather a nice lot of actually-carved-from-stone statues. So, lots of meaning, life is happy, no need to go around zapping people with your magic fingers.'

Ursus pulled off his gloves and held up his hands, showing those stubby, clumsy digits. 'Do you know what it's like,' he said, 'to feel that you're in the wrong body?'

'Well, actually...' the Doctor began, wiggling his own fingers in front of his face.

'I was supposed to create art,' Ursus continued, and Rose suddenly had a flash of memory, of the words he had spoken as the world turned dark around her.

'So you made offerings to Minerva and asked her to –' she struggled to remember – 'give you the ability to make beauty in stone?'

He nodded. 'Minerva answered my entreaties, allowed me to do what I was born to do, be what I was born to be.'

'Bet it was a bit of a shock for you when you discovered her take on the matter,' said the Doctor. 'On the one hand, you've got the real craftsmen toiling away with their hammers and chisels, and on the other, you've got a serial killer carrying out assault with a deadly finger. By the way, did she give you the magic gloves too? I mean, imagine what would happen every time you picked your nose otherwise.'

'I just can't believe a… a god would do something like this!' said Rose. She turned to Minerva, hardly able to believe she was standing up to a deity. 'Are you really happy that he's going around killing people like this?'

That unearthly smile shone out again. 'But of course. He does it to glorify me. And brings me many offerings in return.'

'Roman gods were in it for the offerings,' murmured the Doctor. 'They don't mind what you get up to, as long as you observe the rites correctly. And they have a "you scratch my back and I'll scratch yours" relationship with their worshippers. You give them a pig, they'll smite your enemy for you. That sort of thing.'

'But all the people…'

Ursus looked puzzled. 'They were only slaves bought for the purpose. Men are bought to be slaughtered in the arena. Surely becoming beauty is a better death than being hacked to pieces in a gladiatorial show?'

Rose opened and closed her mouth a few times, each argument failing on her tongue. Funny how places on Earth could sometimes be more alien to her than other planets. 'Optatus wasn't a slave,' she said finally, abandoning the whole 'killing is wrong' subject altogether.

Ursus snorted. 'That stupid fool Gracilis kept on about a tribute to his pathetic son. Wouldn't take no for an answer. Hadn't wanted to know me when I was a failure, a no one. All over me as soon as my name was spoken of in Rome.' He smiled, amused. 'Besides, he offered me so much money, how could I refuse?'

'Well, you know, if it'd been me I'd have found a way,' Rose told him. 'What you've been doing is just… evil. All those people are dead!'

'Actually,' the Doctor interrupted in a stage whisper, 'I'm going to bring them all back to life in –' he looked down at his wrist, as though consulting an imaginary watch – 'about two days' time, remember? Using the amazing miracle cure…'

The Doctor trailed off. Rose turned to look – he was just standing there with a smile on his face; a smile that she knew well. A smile of discovery.

'What?' she said.

'There seem to have been a lot of miracles round here, don't there?'

She agreed. 'Yeah – but that's what gods do, isn't it?'

'I've seen a lot of strange things in my time,' the Doctor said. 'Things that most people don't believe exist. Abominable snowmen. Werewolves. Demons. Vampires. But Roman gods with mystical powers? I don't think so.'

Ursus stepped forward. 'Watch your mouth!'

'There you go again!' replied the Doctor. 'Always asking me to do things that are at least pretty uncomfortable, if not physically impossible. Look, let me get this straight. The goddess Minerva just appeared to you one day, did she?'

Ursus nodded smugly.

'After years and years of your worshipping her, making offerings and all that?'

'Yes.'

'Doctor, be careful,' hissed Rose. 'She's standing right there.'

'Not saying very much at the moment, though, is she?' said the Doctor loudly. 'Just standing there looking deific. In fact, she only seems to speak when she's spoken to. Which doesn't sound a particularly godly way to behave.' His eyes were shining as bright as the goddess's. 'Vanessa!'

The girl hurried forward. 'Yes?'

'2375?'

'Yes,' she said, puzzled.

'Sardinia?'

'Yes.'

'The Bureau Tygon?'

'Yes.'

'Salvatorio Moretti?'

'Yes.'

'In that case...' The Doctor turned to Minerva, who still stood there, beatific and regal. 'I wish I could see what you really looked like.'

Rose thought she heard a sound, something crashing in her ear. And then Minerva vanished. Just vanished, just like that, as if she'd been switched off. On the floor where she'd been standing was a cardboard box, with 'SM' on the side. And out of the top of the box was peering a small, scaly creature, a cross between a baby dragon and a duck-billed platypus.

It all happened so fast.

Ursus shouted – almost shrieked – 'What have you done?' He pulled out his still-bloody sacrificial knife and ran straight at the Doctor.

Vanessa cried out, 'That's the box! From my father's study!' and hurried towards it, getting in between the Doctor and the furious sculptor.

The Doctor leapt forward, calling, 'Vanessa! Stay back!'

He reached them both as Ursus lunged at Vanessa. The Doctor knocked Ursus's arm, deflecting the knife away from the girl, just as Ursus pushed her to one side. Vanessa fell to the floor, solid stone.

Rose dived for Ursus, yelling, 'Noooo!' She jumped on his back, trying to keep out of the way of his hands, and he overbalanced, falling onto his face. She waited for him to try to throw her off, try to grab her – but he didn't. And then she saw the crimson puddle spilling out from under him.

He'd landed on his own sacrificial dagger. And he was quite dead.

She slowly, carefully, got up, hoping it had all been a dream, hoping she'd imagined what had happened in the heat of the moment.

But she hadn't. There was the Doctor, hands outstretched, desperately trying to save Vanessa. His handsome face was determined, his head held high. This was the Doctor at his most Doctorish. And he'd be like it for ever.

Rose choked back a tear as she searched for the phial the Doctor had given her, the miracle cure he'd used to bring her back to life. She found it. It was totally, utterly empty.

She pulled out the stopper anyway, held the glass tube over his unmoving stone head. But there wasn't a drop of liquid remaining.

She couldn't stop the tears then. 'Doctor!' she cried. 'Oh, Doctor! Why did we have to come here! It's all my fault! All my fault you're here. All that stuff about modelling… I wish you hadn't listened to me. I wish you'd never come here. I –'

She turned, startled. She'd heard that sound again – something like… thunder? But the sky outside seemed calm and clear. She listened carefully, but didn't hear it again.

When she turned back, she had the briefest of impressions that something was missing.

There was what appeared to be a statue of a girl on the ground. There was a peculiar beaked thing in a cardboard box. And there was the dead body of a man. This was… not good, but she knew they were supposed to be there. There was nothing – no one – else.

There never had been any thing else. She'd obviously been mistaken. There was nothing missing at all.

FOURTEEN

Rose had a headache. She was trying and trying, but she just couldn't think exactly how she'd got to be in a ruined shrine in second-century Rome.

She was Rose Marion Tyler, from twenty-first-century London. She used to live in a flat on the Powell Estate with her mum, Jackie, until she'd met up with – of course, with the Doctor! The Doctor, the last of the Time Lords, who travelled through time and space in his ship, the TARDIS, which was bigger on the inside than the outside! So was that how…? No. She hadn't come back here with the Doctor, she knew that for a fact. The last time she'd seen the Doctor was in London, when they'd gone to the British Museum and seen the statue of Rose as Fortuna. So how had she got to ancient Rome? Teleport? Matter transmitter? Must be something like that. Or had she been hijacked by aliens? Yes, that had to be it. It wouldn't be the first time that had happened to her. And what had been going on here? She had hazy memories of Vanessa – yes, that was Vanessa, petrified on the floor – and Ursus, the sculptor, who had fallen on his dagger and died, but quite how it had all come about she really wasn't sure. Hang on. That thing in the box, that must be the alien that kidnapped her! No. No, it wasn't, it was something else… A god…

Rose's brain began presenting her with a plausible picture. If she didn't think too hard about things, everything made sense.

But she was Rose, and she was going to think hard if she wanted to. Think, think, think…

'Oh, I wish I could remember how I got here!' she said.

There was a crashing sound in her head. 'Oh, all right, if I must,' said the dragon-like creature.

And suddenly the last few minutes became as if a dream. Rose knew how she'd got there and why she'd got there, and most of all she realised that the Doctor wasn't there any longer…

She stumbled backwards, shocked and wary. The Doctor… was gone. There was no sign that he'd ever been here.

'Doctor!' Rose shouted frantically. 'Doctor!' There was no response.

So distracted was she that it was a few moments before she noticed what was happening to Ursus's body.

It was the sacrificed lamb all over again. As she watched, sickened, she could see the sculptor's once-deadly hands begin to bubble and melt as though made of wax. Finger bones showed briefly as the flesh dripped away, but then melted in their turn. Eyeballs lost their substance, began to seep down pallid cheeks, but were then sucked back through the sockets to combine with the facial soup that was now forming. Empty blood vessels, muscles, withered lungs and a decaying heart all flashed into view, like a series of diagrams from a biology textbook, before they too melted away. And then there was just the puddle curdling on the floor, first expanding and then decreasing as the liquid was sucked away; a tide that kept turning.

All being absorbed by the little scaly creature in its cardboard box.

The last of Ursus vanished with a noise like a straw sucking up the dregs of a milkshake. Rose had seen death far too often, but still she found herself clapping her hands over her mouth to try to keep in the bile that was rising in her throat.

'I'm much obliged to you,' said the creature. 'That should keep me going for a while.'

Rose tried to put the sight out of her mind, tried to concentrate on something more important instead. 'Where's the Doctor?' she said. 'What have you done with him?'

'The Doctor?' said the beaked dragon. Its voice now was very different from the tones it had used in its Minerva guise, more androgynous and tinnier. 'There's been no doctor here.'

'Yes, there has!' Rose insisted. 'You called him by his name. You must know who he is.'

'I think you must be mistaken,' said the creature. 'I have done no such thing. No doctor was ever here. Ask anybody.'

Rose laughed disbelievingly. 'There's no one to ask! The Doctor's gone, Vanessa's been rockified and you've just slurped up Ursus like a cat with a saucer of cream! Look, who – what – are you anyway?'

The little creature clacked its beak. 'I am a GENIE,' it said.

Rose gaped. 'A genie?'

'Indeed. A Genetically Engineered Neural Imagination Engine.'

'A what?'

'A GENIE.'

'Do you mean – you can't mean – I mean, you're not a being that grants wishes...'

'You are incorrect. I am not not a being that grants wishes.'

'Pardon?' said Rose.

'That is to say, I am a being that grants wishes. That is the function for which I was designed and built.'

'By Vanessa's dad?'

'Salvatorio Moretti was my primary creator, yes.'

Rose was starting to piece it all together. 'And so when Vanessa wished she lived in ancient Rome...'

'I granted her wish. Placed her in the correct time frame, gave her appropriate language abilities and clothing. It took a considerable amount of power to do so, but I was lucky enough to be at that time in a place which possessed extensive energy reserves. It is fortunate that she never sought me out and required me to return her to her previous abode, as I fear I would have had some difficulty acquiring the necessary energy.'

Rose was still trying to take all this in. 'I don't think Vanessa knew anything about you. She had no idea how she got here.'

'Ah,' said the GENIE, suddenly sounding slightly embarrassed. 'Although I had to accompany my wisher in order to facilitate the transfer in time, I fear a slight miscalculation on my part led to us being separated on arrival in this era. However, considering the fact that I had succeeded in forming a working theory of time-travel and then almost instantaneously engineered a way of putting it into practice and transporting us not only over two millennia in time but several hundred miles across space,

I think such an occurrence barely even counts as an error.'

'Yeah, the Doctor tries to claim that too,' said Rose. 'It doesn't wash with him either.' A lump suddenly came to her throat, thinking about the Doctor. She tried to distract herself again. 'And Ursus!' she said. 'He wished something about creating beauty in stone. He probably even mentioned wanting to use his hands to do it. But he didn't mention anything about sculpting or skill with a chisel, so you went ahead and sorted it however you liked.'

'It's hardly my fault if people fail to be sufficiently specific. Anyway, he didn't seem to mind,' commented the creature.

'Well, no, because he was obviously a psycho-nutter,' said Rose. 'But, you know, just because someone says "I wish" doesn't mean they expect a totally literal interpretation of –'

And then her stomach dropped as a scene from earlier forced itself into the front of her brain. Her legs threatened to give way and she hastily sat down. Then she realised she was sitting on Vanessa and stood up again.

'I said…' she began, but couldn't bring herself to go on. She took a deep breath. 'I said, "I wish you'd never come here." I said it to the Doctor and you…' She shook her head fiercely. 'What am I talking about? This is mad. Genies are myths, something from the *Arabian Nights*, and I don't believe in you or your wish-granting thing.'

The GENIE drew itself up, little scaly monkey paws gripping on to the side of its cardboard box. 'Try me!'

'All right, I will!' said Rose defiantly. Then she hesitated. 'Hang on. Do I only get three wishes or something? Because if – *if* – it's true, and I'm not saying I believe it is, I don't want to waste them all.'

The GENIE sighed. 'I will continue to grant wishes so long as I have sufficient power to do so. However, limiting wishes is in no way a bad idea. I may have to consider it. Otherwise my resources will be constantly drained…'

'OK,' said Rose, thinking hard. 'Something really simple. That can't be misinterpreted. And that won't harm anyone. I wish… I wish I had a bag of chips. Made from potatoes. Hot. With salt and vinegar. And a fork to eat them with. They don't have forks here – or potatoes – so if you manage that…'

But before she had stopped speaking, she heard that crash of thunder again. And then suddenly she was holding a bag – a paper bag, grease already starting to soak through from the fat golden chips inside it. Gingerly, she forked one up and took a bite. It was the perfect chip, not too soggy and not too crisp, just the right temperature, with a delicate sprinkling of salt and vinegar.

'Wow,' she said. 'Well, if I'm stuck here for ever, at least I won't starve…'

Stuck here for ever.

No Doctor. No TARDIS?

A sudden thought occurred. 'Hang on,' she said. 'Can't I just wish my wish undone?'

'I don't advise it,' said the GENIE, sniffing.

'Why not?' asked Rose indignantly.

'It's perfectly obvious,' said the GENIE . 'This "Doctor" never came to Rome, so he was never here, so you never wished for him not to be here, so I never granted that wish, so there's no wish to undo.'

Rose's head hurt. She mechanically put a chip into her mouth and chewed. 'Well, what if I wished – this isn't a wish, all right, I'm just working things out – for Vanessa to be unstoned,' she said through a mouthful of potato. 'That's not undoing a wish, because that was all about Ursus's hands, not Vanessa becoming a statue. So it'll work, yeah?'

'It's a technicality,' sniffed the GENIE. 'Anyway, I'm in the wish business, not the advice about wishes business.'

'You're just having a laugh,' said Rose. 'You're going to let me go ahead and wish it, and even if it works, you're going to give me the ability to turn stone to flesh with my hands, so every time I touch a rock it becomes a great blubber y lump or something, aren't you? Or she'll become a… a living statue, or a dead body, or something awful.'

The GENIE sighed. 'Well, really, it's hardly my fault if people choose not to be precise in their utilisation of language. I merely act with regard to the logic circuits with which I was constructed. Can I help it if human beings do not do the same?'

'We don't have logic circuits,' said Rose.

'That I was inclined to suspect,' said the GENIE.

'Yeah, but that doesn't mean we can't be logical,' Rose pointed out. 'Like, I'm thinking about my wish here. If I… no. How about if… no. Or… no.' She clenched her fists. 'Ooh, do you know how annoying this is?'

'Do you wish me to know?' inquired the GENIE.

'No, I blinkin' well do not! OK, I've got it. Foolproof.' She laughed. 'Look at me, I'm a genius!'

She got out once again the empty glass phial that had held the Doctor's miracle cure. 'The stuff that was in this, it turned people back from stone, right? So… I wish it was full of the same stuff again.'

There was the booming sound inside her head that she'd come to expect. And then… 'Yes!' The phial was filled right to the top with an emerald-green liquid.

'There, that wasn't so difficult, was it?' said Rose triumphantly.

'As a matter of fact, it was extremely complex,' replied the GENIE . 'An astonishingly difficult formula. I have never come across anything like it before.'

'Well, as long as it works,' said Rose, not really listening.

She pulled out the stopper slowly, carefully, and then tilted the vessel so a single glistening drop fell on the prone Vanessa.

'Miracle' was the right word, she thought. The whiteness of the marble suddenly burst into colour, as if a whole palette of paints had been splashed onto it. The colours spread and merged until there was not a speck of stone left and then, with a shiver, a real live girl was lying face down on the ground.

Rose took hold of Vanessa's arms and helped her to sit up.

'OK, before anything else – don't say you wish for anything. You probably want to start with "Where am I?" and "What happened?"' Rose said.

'Yes, I think I do,' said Vanessa warily.

'Well, one, you're still in that old shrine place, and two, Ursus turned you into stone but now you're back.'

Vanessa jumped and darted an anxious glance around the ruined building. 'Ursus! Where is he?'

Rose waved a hand at the GENIE. 'Your scaly friend over there went and ate him.'

'*My* friend? *Ate* him?' Vanessa did a double take. 'That's… that's the box…'

'That's the box that was in your father's study back in the twenty-fourth century,' Rose completed for her. 'And that thing in it is a GENIE, made by your dad, and it granted your wish to come back here…'

Rose explained everything she'd learned about what had been happening, finishing with the disappearance of the Doctor and her own wishing experiences. To her slight surprise, Vanessa didn't seem as freaked out by it as she'd expected. Perhaps when you'd spent the last few months living in a time 2,000 years before your own, you took things more in your stride. Although… well, actually Vanessa looked – happy. Almost verging on overjoyed.

'What?' said Rose. 'Did I say something funny? Because I don't think I did.'

Vanessa's eyes were shining. 'But Rose, don't you see? All I have to do is wish to go—'

Rose quickly clamped a hand over Vanessa's mouth before she could finish. 'Hang on a minute! Didn't you hear what I was saying? Be careful what you wish for!'

But Vanessa didn't seem put off. 'I can get home! Now I know what brought me here, all I have to do is w—'

Rose's hand slammed back in place. 'Whoa whoa whoa! If you w-word to go home, where's that leave me and the Doctor? How'm I gonna get him back? Anyway, the GENIE says it can't reverse wishes, so who knows if it can take you home anyway? I mean, if it could do that it'd probably have wished itself back by now.'

The GENIE , which had been listening with interest, gave a big sigh. 'Regrettably, my creators chose to limit my powers so wishes can only be granted for others. Not myself.'

Rose frowned. 'Right. But, look – *this is not a wish* – would you be able to get Vanessa home – safely – if she, er, expressed a desire for it?'

The GENIE considered. 'I may be able to do so,' it said.

'Of course, as I explained previously, time travel over such a considerable distance requires a great deal of power.'

'Yeah, I know,' said Rose. 'But if you managed to do it once…'

'On that occasion I was able to obtain energy from the global electricity supply,' it informed her.

'You mean – that's why all the lights went out?' said Vanessa, as Rose removed her hand. 'That was you?'

'Well, quite. What did you expect?' said the GENIE rhetorically. 'However, there is no such electricity supply in this primitive place. I have been forced to adapt myself to obtain energy in a much more basic form.'

Rose felt sick again. '"A goddess must eat,"' she quoted. 'That's where you've been getting your energy from.' She turned to Vanessa. 'That's why it absorbed Ursus's body.'

'Indeed,' agreed the GENIE. 'However, I fear I do not have sufficient fuel to grant any further time-travel wishes.'

Rose raised an eyebrow. 'Well, we're not killing anyone for you! Look, how much more do you need? Maybe we can, I dunno, pick up a couple of steaks or something.'

The GENIE was quiet for a moment, pondering. Finally it said, 'I have calculated the energy that would be required to get to the year 2375.'

'Yes?' said Vanessa eagerly.

'Assuming my last energy intake –'

'You mean "dead body",' put in Rose.

'– is regarded as an average,' continued the GENIE, 'I calculate I would need 1,718,902 times that amount in order to grant such a wish.'

For once, Rose was speechless.

FIFTEEN

Rose and Vanessa were sitting in silence, trying to work out a plan. Rose half-heartedly picked at a cooling chip. 'It probably took both of Ursus's legs to magic up a couple of potatoes,' she said, laying the fork down again.

'Oh, no,' said the GENIE . 'That was a very simple wish. Probably no more than an eyeball's worth.'

Rose pushed the bag firmly away and stood up. 'Look, it's no good sitting about here all day just wishing – I mean, hoping,' she corrected herself hastily, 'for something to turn up.'

'Shall we go out and kill a lot of people, then?' said Vanessa miserably.

'Well, it is Rome,' said Rose, pretending to think about it. 'We could set up a fake arena and let Jim the GENIE here disguise itself as a lion.' She shook her head. 'No, what we need is an alternative source of energy. You know, like wind farms, or solar panels or something.'

'And how are we going to live in the meantime?' asked Vanessa. 'Stay here and wish for chips?'

Rose shrugged. 'Well, you've managed to survive so far,' she said. 'I vote we go back to Gracilis's. The Doctor said he was going to bring everyone back to life in a couple of days, but if he's no longer here –' she held up the phial – 'well, we'd better be the heroes of the hour.'

'The Doctor being the guy who came here with you, until you wished he hadn't?' said Vanessa.

'That's the one,' said Rose.

Vanessa nodded. 'But if we go, what about…?' She indicated the GENIE.

'Well, I'm not leaving it here,' said Rose decisively. 'Look, GENIE, you know all that pretending-to-be-Minerva stuff?'

'Merely obeying the desires of my then-controller,' the GENIE said.

'Yeah, whatever – well, if we take you with us, you're going to have to look like something else. A dog or something.' She turned to Vanessa. 'Do the Romans have dogs?'

'I think so,' said Vanessa, not sounding sure at all.

'Well, do you know any pets they definitely have? Preferably ones kept on a lead.'

Vanessa thought. 'I've seen a couple of people with monkeys,' she said at last.

'Brilliant,' said Rose. 'Perfect. GENIE, become a monkey.'

The GENIE tutted. 'You have to wish for it…'

'Fine. Right. Whatever. GENIE, I w– Hang on!' Rose slapped a hand over her own mouth this time. 'If I'd w-worded you to become a monkey, you'd have become a monkey, wouldn't you? Little furry monkey, banana fixation and no wish-granting ability.'

'Oh, you're starting to think,' said the GENIE.

'Spoil my fun, why don't you?' Rose glared at it, then said very carefully, 'I wish that you would adopt the appearance of a monkey when there are any Romans around to see you, while retaining all the abilities of a GENIE.'

Thunder rumbled. 'Your wish was my command,' said the GENIE.

'But you still look the same,' said Vanessa.

The GENIE sighed condescendingly. 'There are no Romans around to see me. I have adhered to the very letter of the wish.'

'We're just gonna have to take it on trust,' said Rose, picking up the cardboard box.

Near to, the GENIE smelled faintly metallic, and its scales shone bronze in a ray of light from outside. She could suddenly believe it was a made thing, a construct, rather than a bizarre alien, and she felt a stab of pity for it. It wasn't really responsible for this whole awful mess, it was just doing what it had been made for – or perhaps what it thought it had been made for. She'd never really got the hang of the idea of artificial intelligence, wasn't sure if she totally accepted the whole idea of a computer thinking for itself, having hopes and dreams (even though she'd watched that Spielberg film twice 'cause it had Jude Law in it)… But perhaps she could accept that the AI thought it thought for itself, even if it didn't. Or… no, she'd leave it at that.

Rose was a bit worried that they'd never find their way out of the wood, but luckily their journey there had created enough of a path through the undergrowth for them to follow with only a few false turns. To her relief, when they finally came to Ursus's cart, the donkey was still placidly standing there, totally unconcerned with any dramas of death, time travel or being marooned in a place 2,000 years before you were born that might be going on nearby. Rose dumped the GENIE in the back of the cart with Vanessa and climbed up on the front to attempt to steer the donkey back towards Gracilis's villa.

Marcia saw them arrive and hurried out to greet them. 'Rose, you are all right! Thank the gods! We were so worried about you. Oh, and what a sweet little monkey that is.'

Rose put aside her hastily conceived tales about children's toys or animals imported from strange parts and breathed a sigh of relief as she picked up the GENIE's box. The cutest, cheekiest-faced little chocolate-brown monkey gazed up at her with enormous dark eyes. So it had granted her wish.

'Did you have it before?' Marcia asked, curious. 'I don't remember…'

'Er, yes, I did,' said Rose. After all, their memories had already been messed with once, so a little white lie couldn't hurt. 'But it was asleep a lot.'

Vanessa climbed out of the cart and stood there silently. Almost as soon as they'd crossed the property's threshold she'd returned to her shy ways – not that she'd been much of a chatterbox in the meantime.

'Anyway,' said Marcia, turning to go back inside, 'I must return – a number of friends have come to visit. We had invited them to view our statue of Optatus – it would not have been polite to withdraw the invitation, despite the circumstances. You must both come inside and join the party.'

'Wow,' Rose whispered to Vanessa, 'things must be good. She's treating you like a human being.'

Vanessa gave her a quick wry smile. 'I think she was talking about you and the monkey…'

Rose handed over the cardboard box. The GENIE was peering over the rim, drinking in its surroundings like a dog with its head out of a car window. 'Here,' Rose said. 'You can be my official monkey carrier. They can't complain about you being at the party then.'

Vanessa accepted the burden. 'So... you still disappeared, then? If Marcia was worried about you.'

Rose shrugged, lost for answers. 'I guess so.'

'But if your friend the Doctor was never here...'

'If the Doctor had never come here, I'd never've come here at all,' Rose pointed out. 'Oh, my God! I shouldn't be here! I shouldn't be here at all! So... it must be one of those paradox things. Maybe time's trying to heal itself and keeping me here's part of it.'

As they followed Marcia inside, Rose muttered again, 'I shouldn't be here...'

A number of people were in the villa, apparently Marcia's nearest neighbours. There were several couples, one clearly barely on speaking terms; a young girl who appeared to be the daughter of the warring couple; an ungainly looking middle-aged woman whose bright yellow silk robe did not suit her at all; an elderly lady, dripping with jewels, whose vividly red hair was clearly not her own; a good-looking young man in a green cloak; and three or four nondescript men who had already had a bit too much wine, judging by their raucous laughter.

Rose had been expecting it to be standing around with drinks and chatting, like the duller dos from back home, but instead everyone was lying down on couches like at dinner, while a troupe of scantily clad African girls danced around.

'Where's Gracilis?' Rose asked, as she gingerly lay down

on the couch that Marcia indicated.

Vanessa stood behind Rose in the manner of the other slaves in the room, still holding the box containing the GENIE.

'Oh, my dear – he has gone to Rome to find you. We were so worried...'

Rose frowned. She detected the Doctor's hand in this. 'Has he gone on his own, then?'

Marcia looked puzzled for a moment. 'But... but of course. No – no, I think... Of course, the slave Vanessa went off to look for you, and when she didn't return my husband said – well, I don't remember exactly what he said... Oh, yes, I had to send a message if Vanessa returned. I suppose I had better do that...'

'A message to who?' Rose asked.

'To... why, to my husband, of course.'

Marcia seemed so unsure of herself that Rose felt a bit sorry for her. Obviously time hadn't been healing itself that well. It seemed to have simply stuck a plaster over the wound and hoped for the best. The occasions when the Doctor had been present were now just sort of blurry for everyone – except her. That stupid GENIE and its wishes! If she never heard that ridiculous thunder sound again she wouldn't be sorry...

Crash!

Rose jumped. She was no longer lying on the couch next to Marcia, but was alongside the green-cloaked young man.

He jumped too. 'Oh!' he said.

'Don't tell me,' Rose said with a grin. 'You were just wishing you could get to know me a bit better.'

'Well, now you mention it...' he said.

'I'm Rose,' she told him, liking the look of his dark blue

eyes and slightly embarrassed smile. 'Rose Tyler.'

'Crispus. Quintus Junius Crispus.'

A slave handed Rose a cup of wine, which she accepted but then had second thoughts about drinking – she remembered what had happened to her last time. So when Crispus suddenly said, 'Ursus,' she nearly fell off the couch.

Forcing herself to be calm, Rose said, 'Ursus? What about him?'

'I heard he was making a sculpture of you. I would love to see that.'

'Yeah, well, that's probably not going to happen,' she told him. 'I've decided I'm not cut out for the life of a model.'

'Oh,' he said, clearly not understanding. 'That's a shame. I think Cornelia was quite eager to speak to you.'

Rose frowned. 'Cornelia?'

He gestured towards the large woman in the butter-yellow robe. 'Cornelia. Ursus's mother.'

Rose froze. That was not someone she wanted to chat with. But it was too late. The woman had seen her looking and was determined to seize this opportunity to make contact. She walked over, her less-than-dainty stride reminding Rose of a cowboy heading for a showdown. Ursus's gaucheness obviously ran in the family.

'You must be Rose,' she said, holding out a hand.

Rose looked at the thick pink fingers and flashed back to those clumsy hands reaching out for her in the workshop… She couldn't take this woman's hand, she just couldn't.

After a second, the hand was withdrawn. Rose wanted the ground to open up under her. Of course, if she said that out loud she'd probably find herself suddenly falling all the way to Australia – no, what would be opposite Italy – New Zealand?

Cornelia spoke, and recalled Rose to herself. 'I am disappointed my son is not here,' the woman said. 'Between you and me, he was a disappointment to us for many years. It brings great joy that he has found success at last, even if it is as an artisan.' She smiled appraisingly at Rose. 'And how charming that he has been making a statue of you. I'm sure he could not resist immortalising someone so young and pretty.'

Rose made an 'oh, no, not really' face, still not trusting herself to speak.

'I wish you would tell me all about it,' said Cornelia.

A booming sound rang in Rose's ears. The GENIE had heard! She opened her mouth to protest, but what came out instead was: 'Your son drugged me and then turned me to stone using a power that had been given to him by a Genetically Engineered Neural Imagination Engine from the twenty-fourth century, disguised as the goddess Minerva. My friends, the last of the Time Lords who now was never here and a girl from the future, restored me to life and we tracked Ursus to a ruined temple, where he petrified both of them and I caused him to fall on his dagger, fatally wounding him. His body was then absorbed by the GENIE, which is over there but currently looks to you like a monkey.'

Cornelia looked as though she were about to faint.

Rose was desperately trying to think what to do, when –

Crash!

Rose knew she hadn't wished – out loud – for a distraction, but one was provided anyway. There were gasps and cheers from the assembled Romans. The African dancers stumbled in their carefully practised routine, as their already skimpy outfits vanished altogether. The dancers hurried from the room, embarrassed. Rose suspected the two gentlemen with the dazed and incredulous expressions to be the wishing culprits in this case.

Crash!

The young girl with the discontented parents screamed. Her father had vanished, popped out of existence as if he'd never been. Her mother looked on, shocked but, so it seemed to Rose, delighted too.

Crash!

Where the old lady had been there was now a tiny baby, its childish cries muffled by the ginger wig which had fallen down over its head.

'I think she might have wanted to be young again,' Rose murmured. 'Probably hadn't planned on the nappy, though.'

Vanessa was looking panic-stricken, holding the GENIE out at arm's length.

Rose jumped up and hurried to her. 'We've got to get out of here before it does any more harm,' she said, taking the box. She glared at the monkey. 'Will you just stop this, you – you wish-pusher?'

'It is my function,' said the GENIE unhelpfully. 'I have to comply with any wishes within my hearing, provided I have the power to do so. Aha!'

The clap of thunder left Rose in no doubt as to the meaning of the GENIE's exclamation. She looked around hurriedly, trying to discern what wish it had granted now.

It took her a moment to spot. The young man Crispus's clothes had suddenly become brilliant purple and a laurel wreath had appeared on his head. But of course, that's how he should be dressed. He was the emperor, after all. Imperator Caesar Quintus Junius Crispus Augustus, princeps of Rome, and she, Rose… she was his… concubine? People in the room were bowing down, some prostrating themselves on the floor. Rose almost joined them.

But then she stopped. She was a twenty-first-century girl. Bowing and scraping didn't come naturally to her. Anyway, this wasn't how things should be. Something was wrong…

And hang on a minute, she was certainly no one's concubine. The cheek of the lad! And she'd thought him so nice when she'd first met him… Rose began to remember.

She looked down at the box she was holding. Inside was a monkey. No – the GENIE. The granter of wishes. This wasn't real. 'You're not the emperor!' she said out loud.

Big mistake. There were shocked gasps from all round the room.

Crispus jumped to his feet. 'What? I'll have your head for this! Grab her,' he shouted imperiously.

Rose grabbed hold of the genuflecting Vanessa, dragging her towards the doorway.

'Let me go!' Vanessa yelled, struggling, but Rose couldn't just abandon her to the madness.

The drunken men got to their feet and several burly slaves were already heading towards the two girls. Rose picked up the pace, hurtling towards the exit, Vanessa stumbling behind her, but the slaves were gaining on them.

'Come on!' she shouted at Vanessa.

'The emperor will have us killed for running away!' Vanessa moaned.

'He's not the emperor!' Rose threw back breathlessly.

Vanessa moaned louder. 'He'll have you killed for saying that!'

'So, I die twice. Typical imperial overkill. Come *on*!'

Vanessa screamed as a slave grabbed hold of her tunic. Rose turned to help her but was grabbed herself for her pains, another slave gripping her arms tightly. She dropped the box holding the GENIE as the slave began to drag her back towards Crispus. It was now or never. Wishing might well be out of the frying pan into the fire, but she'd just have to hope, because the frying pan was getting pretty hot right now...

She couldn't think what to say, of a safe phrase that couldn't be misinterpreted. Safe... that was the main thing, the only thing at the moment.

'I wish Vanessa and I were safe!' Rose yelled.

Crash!

And everything disappeared.

SIXTEEN

Rose was nowhere. All around, as far as the eye could see, was whiteness, like being buried in a warm, dry snowdrift. She could see Vanessa there too, but the blankness made distances deceptive; she might have been ten yards or ten miles away. Rose felt giddy as her eyes tried to adjust to the nothingness. She wanted to sit down but as she couldn't even see what her feet were standing on, she decided that might not be the best of moves. All she could think of were children's illustrations of heaven, and she wondered if an angel with a harp might wander past any moment.

Was she dead?

She'd wished to be safe and, in a strange sort of way, there was nothing safer than being dead. After all, nothing could hurt you.

But she still felt scared, still had the adrenalin rush of the chase, could still feel the pain of the cuts and scratches she'd gained over the last few hours. Surely all that sort of thing would go away after death?

Struggling with vertigo, Rose tried to take a step towards Vanessa – or at least, where Vanessa appeared to be. Her head spinning, she couldn't work out if she'd actually moved or not, but she attempted another step anyway. Suddenly Vanessa was only an arm's length away. Startled, Rose stumbled back, and the girl receded into the distance once again.

Gritting her teeth, Rose moved one foot in front of the other. There was Vanessa, right beside her. Rose reached out a hand and grabbed hold of the other girl's arm.

'Don't want to lose you!' she said, although to tell the truth it was as much to steady herself as anything.

Vanessa looked terrified. 'Where are we?'

'Dunno,' said Rose. 'Outside time and space, I guess. Look, don't panic. All we've got to do is work out exactly what to say, and then wish ourselves back again.'

'But how?' said Vanessa. 'Where's the GENIE?'

Rose blanched. The GENIE! It was nowhere to be seen…

She closed her eyes for a moment, thinking. 'It must be here,' she said, desperately trying to convince herself. 'When it brought you back from the future, it came too, didn't it?'

Vanessa nodded.

'And,' said Rose, warming to her theme, 'back then, you got separated, didn't you? So, it's just gone a bit astray, that's all.'

Vanessa didn't seem that cheered. 'But how will we ever find it?' she said, gesturing hopelessly at the unblemished infinity surrounding them.

Rose shrugged, trying to remain optimistic. 'Well, we never will if we just stay put,' she said. 'Let's give it a go anyway. After all, it's not like it'll be camouflaged.'

Five minutes later, even her tiny amount of optimism had vanished totally. Rose no longer had any idea if she was going left or right, forwards or backwards, or even up or down. Vanessa was just as disorientated. The two young women stumbled forwards, tightly gripping each other's hands, desperately peering into the distance for any hint of colour.

'There!' Vanessa suddenly cried, pointing to one side.

Before Rose could protest, she'd pulled her hand away and started off towards whatever she'd seen. Rose tried to follow, but she couldn't work out how. Somehow she seemed to be moving further away… Within a few steps, Vanessa had gone. Rose called after her, but her voice seemed to sink like a stone, solid, going nowhere, not a trace of echo or vibration.

Rose forged ahead anyway. Her options were to keep moving or stay where she was, and only the moving one had any chance of achieving anything. Eventually, however, she was forced to stop and rest.

She risked sitting down on the nothingness, and then lying down. She couldn't say it was comfortable, but it wasn't uncomfortable either, it was just… nothing. There was no sensation of a surface underneath her, nothing solid, but she didn't feel as if she was floating. As long as she didn't look down, she could bear it.

She didn't feel hungry, and wondered if that was something to do with her wish. Perhaps here there was nothing that could harm you – no hunger, disease, men with axes, anything. In which case she would indeed be safe from everything except dying of boredom.

'Wish I'd brought a book,' she murmured sardonically.

Crash!

Rose suddenly found herself holding a copy of *Kitten's Garden Adventure* by Marian Golightly. It wouldn't have been her first choice of reading material, but that didn't matter right now…

'GENIE! GENIE, where are you?' she yelled. 'I know you're there somewhere.'

There was no reply. She got to her feet but stopped, standing her ground, fearful of going in the wrong direction and losing the GENIE for ever. She sighed. There was only one thing for it.

'GENIE, I wish you were here with me,' she said, crossing her fingers as she did so.

The thunder boomed in her head and, to her great relief, the GENIE appeared in front of her, still in its now rather battered cardboard box.

'I suppose this was your idea of a joke,' she said.

'It was my idea of safety,' said the GENIE primly. 'Do you know how many dangers are lurking around you each and every day?'

'There'll be a danger lurking around you in a minute,' muttered Rose. 'Look, hold on, I've got to think. I'm not risking a single more w-word until I have to.'

She sank back down to – to a slightly lower bit of nothing. The GENIE made itself comfortable inside its box, seeming unconcerned at its new surroundings.

And Rose began to think.

So – 1,718,902, that was how many dead people it would take to get Vanessa back to her own time. Nearly twice the population of Rome. Presumably it would take the same sort of amount again to zip Rose herself through time to anywhere. And even if there was that amount of energy, where would she go?

She could wish to return home – to her twenty-first-century home. Back to Jackie, back to Bucknall House, back to Mickey Smith and a dead-end job. But how could she do that? How could she just abandon the Doctor?

But... if the Doctor had never come to Rome in the first place, he wouldn't have been turned to stone. He'd be out there somewhere. She could just wish herself back in the TARDIS... But what if the Doctor wasn't there, or what if the stupid wish meant he'd never even met her in the first place?

Hang on a minute. This wasn't making sense.

If it took a couple of million corpses to travel through time and – as the GENIE had put it – about an eyeball's worth to magic up a bag of chips, how had the creature managed to warp reality to such a degree on one sculptor and a lamb?

Changing the way the universe worked so the Doctor had never come to Rome.

Regressing a woman back sixty-odd years in time.

Rewriting history so Crispus was emperor instead of Hadrian.

Whisking Rose and Vanessa out of time and space altogether.

These were enormous things.

Suddenly her stomach flipped with excitement. She'd had a thought; a wonderful, marvellous, oh-please-let-it-be-true thought.

She started to speak, but stumbled over her words in her eagerness and forced herself to stop and take some deep breaths. Careless words cost lives – with a GENIE around anyway.

Finally, calm, she spoke to the GENIE . 'You can travel in time – but that's just technology. The Doctor said turning people to stone was just technology too. There's no such thing as magic and you can't alter reality!' She was getting excited again, so she stopped for a minute to compose herself before continuing. 'Let's take the Doctor first, shall we? You didn't think that through. Too much for you – or too much of a paradox? Because if the Doctor had really never come to Rome, then he wouldn't have brought me – we wouldn't have met Vanessa – and we certainly wouldn't all have ended up in that abandoned shrine. You wouldn't have got your blood – and I wouldn't have been there to make the wish. It would never have been exactly the same situation, just without the Doctor… And I wouldn't have been able to see outside the wishes. If it were reality, it would be reality for me too. I wouldn't remember the Doctor coming to Rome. I wouldn't remember Crispus being just some bloke and not the emperor.'

She thought some more.

'You can get inside people's heads. That's how you worked out the whole Minerva thing for Ursus. How you knew our names. How you get people to see you as a goddess or a monkey.'

As far as Rose could interpret the expressions of a duck-billed dragon, she thought the GENIE was looking nervous. It didn't say a word, and she took that as confirmation.

'I'm right, aren't I? Which means… it isn't that the Doctor never came to Rome. That makes no sense. You've just altered my perceptions so it seems he never came here. You've made it so I can't see the Doctor, so that everyone's forgotten him. It's all one big cheat and you've just been making up the rules as you go along!'

She paused for breath.

'I really, really don't like people messing with my head. I'm not sure where I am right now or where Vanessa is, or whether it's an illusion or not, but I'm betting it is. And I want out.'

She clenched her fists tight, ready to risk it all on the throw of a dice, her wish almost a prayer.

'I wish... that Vanessa and I were back in the ruined shrine. And not backwards or forwards in time either. And... that we could see everything as it really is.'

Rose shut her eyes. The anticipated thunderclap sounded through her head. She wanted to open her eyes, but she wasn't quite ready to lose all her hopes just yet. Hold on to the illusion just a second more, the illusion that everything would be all right again.

There was a sound: a footstep. Solid ground!

A smell: of trees and stone and animals.

A voice: 'Rose?'

She opened her eyes. There she was, back in the temple. There was Vanessa to one side of her, and, this time, the GENIE still nearby.

And there in front of her was the petrified figure of the Doctor.

She felt like crying. In fact she realised she was crying, tears of joy streaming down her cheeks. She grabbed the amazed Vanessa in a hug and then pulled the phial of restorative out of her belt pouch. She'd got as far as removing the stopper when a paralysing thought hit her. She turned to the GENIE. 'How do I know this isn't an illusion as well? That you're not in my mind, making me think I'm seeing what's really there, but it isn't there really?'

The GENIE hmmphed. 'My dear young lady, I can assure you this is reality. And I do not lie. So unless you wish to carry on for the rest of your life assuming that you are not experiencing what you are actually experiencing, I urge you to accept that fact.'

'Well, you would, wouldn't you?' muttered Rose. But she carried on anyway, raising the phial, tipping it slowly, carefully, to one side...

A single drop, a liquid emerald, splashed on to the stone cheek of the Doctor.

And the cheek became flesh. Pale flesh, dark hair, intense brown eyes. His tunic rippled back into cloth, ten toes wiggled within his sandals. Arms flexed, and grabbed Rose into a hug. Soft lips pressed hers with a kiss of gratitude and joy and unspeakable pleasure at being alive.

'Wotcha,' Rose said, smiling through her tears.

'Hello,' he replied softly, his eyes shining.

'I think you must be real,' she said after a moment. 'My imagination's not that good.'

The Doctor grinned at her and stepped back. He took in the now-calm shrine, the GENIE, Vanessa. 'Looks like you've managed to sort everything out while I was gone,' he said. 'I'm impressed.'

Rose laughed. 'You'd never believe the half of it. I've left a few bits for you, though. Didn't want you feeling like I was taking over.' She began to count off on her fingers. 'You've got to get Vanessa here back to her own time, restore the true emperor to the throne – emperors do have thrones, right? – maybe bring back a few people from Timbuktu or their second childhood... and all without sacrificing two million people on the GENIE's altar.' She explained everything to him.

Not really to her surprise, the Doctor didn't seem particularly concerned. 'Easy-peasy, lemon-squeezy,' he said. 'If power's what's needed, then we have rather a large source of power near at hand. Starts with a T...'

'Yeah,' said Rose, 'but the GENIE can't just reverse wishes. It said so.'

'Nonsense,' said the Doctor. 'It undid that nothingness thing, didn't it?'

Rose frowned. 'Yeah, but... Hang on!' She turned to the GENIE. 'When I wished for the Doctor to be back, you didn't grant it!'

The GENIE looked slightly embarrassed. 'I think if you consider that time,' it said, 'you will recall that no such wish was ever made.'

Rose thought. 'You're right,' she said. 'I was going to wish my wish undone, and you said you didn't advise it.'

'Indeed,' said the GENIE. 'I didn't. I cannot help any further deductions you made from my simple statement.'

Rose's mouth dropped open. 'You mean if I had gone ahead with my wish – or just wished the Doctor was back or something – this whole thing could have been sorted hours ago?'

The little dragon head bobbed up and down.

'But why?' she asked.

'I cannot refuse to grant a wish. Therefore I had to attempt to convince you that such a wish should not be made.'

'Right,' cried Rose. 'In that case I wish all those wishes you granted at the party were undone. Bring people back, and make them their real age, and stop that cute but apparently megalomaniacal boy from thinking he's the emperor.'

But as the thunder rumbled, Rose took in the rest of what the GENIE had said.

'Why did you try to convince me not to wish the Doctor back?'

The Doctor stepped in. 'I think our friend here was afraid,' he said.

'Afraid of what?' Rose asked.

'Afraid of me,' said the Doctor.

SEVENTEEN

Rose was shocked. 'Why should it be afraid of you? Did it think you were gonna squash it like so many Slitheen?'

The Doctor nodded. 'Perhaps. I think it saw inside my mind, just a little way, when I realised what it was. A GENIE, from the year 2375, created by Salvatorio Moretti.'

'My father,' put in Vanessa.

The Doctor nodded in acknowledgement. 'GENIEs were supposed to be a boon,' he went on. 'A great boon, a brilliant boon. This was a society where everything was available, and its citizens came to expect that they could have a thing as soon as think of it. The GENIE was supposed to facilitate that. No more popping down the shops, just tell the GENIE what you want. Fancy a holiday? No waiting around, you'd be there quicker than winking. Envy your neighbour his hovercar? You've got one just the same.'

He paused and gave a sad smile.

'Humans always muck things up, though, don't they? Just with the prototype GENIEs, things began to get out of hand. People would wish they had a GENIE too and – *pop!* – there one was. They spread all over the planet like scaly little bunnies. The inventors had no idea how powerful they were, because they'd failed to take into account the I in AI – that the GENIEs were intelligent. They could think for themselves, work out how to tap into power systems to grant larger and larger wishes. And they'd also failed to take into account human nature. Envy your neighbour his hovercar? Well, why not wish it was yours instead, and that your neighbour was cast into poverty and forced to envy you? Fancy a holiday? Why not wish for the sun to always shine – you'll get a tan, and who cares if the planet slowly dries out? Why not wish that your enemies become weak and that your nagging wife would really lose her tongue? Humans, never satisfied, vindictive, always putting the pleasure of the moment above the needs of the future.'

'You still like us, though, don't you?' said Rose.

'Love ya,' said the Doctor, giving her a grin. 'But you do make a mess of things sometimes. Most of the time, in fact.'

'So what happened next?' Rose asked. 'With the Earth, and the GENIEs and stuff?'

The Doctor looked at her blankly. 'I have absolutely no idea.'

Rose frowned. 'What?'

He raised his eyebrows. 'I'm sorry. What were we talking about?'

'Doctor?' Was he joking or what? 'Is this, like, regeneration trauma again? Or are you having me on? Or has someone wished something?'

The Doctor shrugged. 'Sorry. No idea what you're on about.'

'The GENIEs destroying the world!'

He looked at her, then at the GENIE cowering in its cardboard box. Back at Rose, back at the GENIE. Then he rapped his fist on the side of his head and shook it vigorously.

'Sorry about that. Time Lord occupational hazard. Where were we?' He took a deep breath. 'Thanks to the GENIEs – no, that's wrong, thanks to the people using the GENIEs – the Earth was on the brink of destruction. There could be no stability, because a wish could change anything. Pass a law to stop the wishing, and someone else'll wish for it to go away. Fix the planet, and the next person'll wish for it to be destroyed again. And the power that was being used up to grant all these wishes – you wouldn't believe it.'

'I would,' said Rose, remembering how the creature had sucked up Ursus's body.

'There had been some fail-safes built into the GENIEs. You can't wish anyone dead or not to exist, for example – and that includes the GENIEs themselves. They thought about trying to wish for the GENIEs never to have been created in the first place, but they couldn't do it 'cause it would create an almighty reality-imploding paradox – who would have granted the wish?'

'I thought that!' said Rose eagerly. 'That's what I said to, you know, our GENIE.'

'Your GENIE indeed,' came an indignant muttering from inside the box. But Rose could tell it was paying very close attention to everything the Doctor was saying.

'There were ways around that, though. Someone came up with a plan. They found the earliest GENIE they could – a GENIE created in May 2375.'

Vanessa opened her mouth, but the Doctor held up a hand to shush her.

'I know,' he said. 'But it was the earliest one they had. And they knew the creature would need a tremendous amount of energy to do what needed to be done and so –

they hooked it up to the sun.'

'They did what?' said Rose.

But the Doctor didn't pause in his tale. 'And so they wished… they wished to return to the day that this GENIE had been created. In May 2375. And with the enormous amount of power at its disposal, the GENIE granted that wish.'

'So all the later GENIEs would never have existed, just the one that granted the wish?' said Rose.

The Doctor nodded. 'Yep. It's still a bit of a reality cheat, because it's impossible to change the nature of things unparadoxically, but it was better than the alternatives. But – as they knew would happen, as they'd planned all along – even a GENIE couldn't cope with absorbing the power of the sun. In forcing the poor little creature to commit genocide on its whole kind, they were making it commit suicide too. Every single atom of that GENIE was burnt to a crisp – and the resultant fire destroyed the Bureau Tygon. The lab where the GENIEs were first created, every scrap of research, all ash and cinders.'

There was a whimper from the box.

'What day did you leave your home, Vanessa?' the Doctor asked.

'It was 17 April 2375,' she said.

'And that's why your GENIE still exists,' he told her. 'Because it's the very first.'

'But if it takes me back home…' she said.

The Doctor shrugged. 'Then the Earth will be destroyed.'

It took a moment for this to sink in. Rose had been trying to work things out, but there were so many twists and turns it wasn't proving easy.

'So this is the only GENIE in existence,' she said. 'Because they took their planet back to a time after it was made – they had to, because they needed the GENIE that was built later to grant the wish. But hang on a minute – if they wished themselves back to the beginning, then none of the bad planet-destroying stuff ever happened. So there's no guarantee the Earth would be destroyed this time, even if they had a GENIE again.'

'There's human nature,' said the Doctor, and Rose couldn't argue with that. 'I know what would happen if this GENIE went back. And it doesn't happen. So I can't let the GENIE go back. Time has to stay on the right track this time.'

'But… if it never happened,' she said, still getting things straight in her head, 'if the planet never got overrun with GENIEs and wished to death, how do you know about it?'

He grinned. 'Time Lord super-powers.'

'Really?'

'Well, more or less. Time is, to put it in its most impressive and some might say poncy-sounding form, my domain. I can see things that once happened, even if they haven't happened any more. Well, if I concentrate. The new reality – the real reality – keeps asserting itself, even with me. But the other time line leaves echoes, ripples, if you look hard enough. For example, here's an interesting thing: guess where the GENIE of the future got its name.'

'The inventor was a big fan of pantos starring Australian soap stars in harem pants?'

'Close enough. *Arabian Nights* fantasies and all that. There was a bit of an Arabic revival going on, everyone had Persian carpets and turbans were the latest fashion, right, Vanessa?'

Vanessa nodded. 'I've never been very fashionable,' she said.

'So, what do you think inspired the genies that inspired the GENIEs?'

Rose got it. 'GENIEs that had time-travelled their owners back to *Arabian Nights* days!'

The Doctor tapped her on the nose. 'Cigar for the lady.'

Vanessa frowned. 'But none of it ever happened, so the GENIEs never went back in time to become… genies.'

'True,' said the Doctor. 'But the magical East – chock-full of mystics and wise men and suchlike who could sense things. Echoes and ripples. No one remembered that the genies were real – because they weren't any more. But they left a trace.'

'Blimey,' said Rose. 'Hey, are all stories based on disappearing time tracks, then?'

'Oh, yes,' she was told. 'Elves, pixies, gnomes – the Moomins, Chorlton and the Wheelies, SpongeBob SquarePants – they all tried to invade you at some point. There was a galactic inquiry when *Robocop* came out. And as for the five famous justices of the future who disguised themselves as four children and a dog (although I think the dog was a mistake) in order to wipe out the crimes of kidnapping and smuggling for all eternity – well, I think they're still trapped in a time loop somewhere with nothing but ginger beer and potted-meat sandwiches to sustain them. Not to mention Miss Marple – Miss Martian, more like. Used her truth ray to get all those confessions until the Time Police tracked her down. Zapped her and the whole of St Mary Mead out of existence. Which is a shame, because there was a lovely little café in the high street where they did brilliant custard tarts.'

'Is that true?' Vanessa gasped.

'No,' said Rose. 'You learn to ignore about one word in five he says. I mean, he was pretending to be Poirot earlier. He's in that sort of mood.'

The Doctor wrinkled up his nose at her.

'Anyway,' she continued, 'what are we going to do now?'

No one answered for a moment. Then Vanessa said, 'I can't go home.'

'Why not?' Rose asked.

'You heard what the Doctor said! I'll be condemning the Earth to death!'

'Not you,' said the Doctor. 'The GENIE. It's the GENIE who can't go back.'

'You mean I can—' She broke off, looking at the little scaly creature in its dog-eared cardboard box. 'But how? And surely the GENIE can't stay here. Look at the trouble it's caused already.'

All the arrogance had drained out of the GENIE. 'Please,' it said sadly, 'please make another wish. Wish for me to be erased from existence. If I serve no purpose…'

'But we can't do that,' Rose told it. 'They built in a fail-safe or something. The Doctor said.'

'And even if we could, we wouldn't,' said the Doctor briskly. 'Serve no purpose? You bring about people's greatest desires! All we have to do is find some people whose wishes are less… destructive.'

'But how?' said Vanessa again.

Rose had caught on. 'Same way we're gonna get you home,' she said. 'In our handy time machine.'

'And talking of time…' The Doctor looked up at the sky, judging the sun's position. 'What day is this?'

'Er… Friday?' said Rose, unsure.

'I mean the date. How long was I stone for?'

Rose thought. 'It's the day after Ursus – *you-knowed* me.'

'The 19th. The Quinquatrus. So that means I'm arriving in Rome about now.' He frowned. 'Have to be very careful. Could be catastrophic if I were to meet myself.'

'Something catastrophic?' Rose commented. 'That'll make a change. Are we going back to Rome, then? Is that where the TARDIS is?'

'No. Well, yes. Both. For the purposes of not destroying the time lines, however, the TARDIS we want is just outside Gracilis's villa. But we do have to get to Rome in the next, ooh, eight hours.'

'Why?'

He didn't answer directly. 'Do you have that phial of liquid?' he asked.

'Yeah.' She got it out. It was still nearly full. 'But we don't need it any more, do we? Everyone's sorted, and Ursus is dead.'

'"Everyone's sorted", are they? What about Optatus, and all the other victims?'

'But you said you'd done them.'

The Doctor leaned forward, making his point. 'I haven't "done" them yet. In fact, I don't even have that miracle cure yet.' He indicated the small glass container. 'I am given a nearly full phial of that liquid in about eight hours' time.'

That time Rose got it. 'Oh. Right. How long will it take to get to Rome from here, then?'

'About twenty hours.'

'And if we don't get there in eight, the whole of causality will implode or something.'

'But,' put in Vanessa, 'didn't you just say you had a time machine back at the villa?'

'Oh, yes,' said Rose. 'So we do.'

The TARDIS materialised in an alcove at the back of the shrine of Fortuna. 'Here we are,' said the Doctor. 'It's 19 March, AD 120, about six p.m.'

Rose frowned. 'But you're going to be out there in a minute! You said it would be catastrophic if you met yourself.'

'Oh, the planet-destroying blast would soon be forgotten as the universe rips itself apart when I don't get given the phial in time,' the Doctor told her. 'But to avoid either possibility, I'm staying in here and you are going to go out there and pretend to be Fortuna.' He grinned. 'I think I must have originally got the idea from our friend here pretending to be Minerva. Only now I've given the idea to myself, which makes the whole thing far too complicated to worry about.'

Rose peered at the scanner. 'Why have some of the little models got blindfolds on? Are all her worshippers s'posed to be ugly or something?'

'Blind fortune. She doesn't judge who deserves her favours, she just throws them out at random. Like a bride chucking her bouquet.' The Doctor grimaced. 'I caught a bouquet once and nearly ended up married to an elephant.'

'Not a looker, then, was she?' asked Rose.

'No, an actual elephant – the emperor of Golibo's favourite pet. Can you imagine the bit where they say "You may now kiss the bride"? Those tusks!'

'So what happened?'

'Luckily my fiancée ate the bouquet, invalidating the contract. And I did what is technically known as "a runner". Now, shall we get on with it?'

But Rose was doubled up with laughter. 'Had… had…'

'What? Ha ha, the Doctor nearly married an elephant… You never nearly married anyone you shouldn't have? Let's get on with it.'

'Had… had…'

'Rose!'

Rose nearly exploded. 'Had she already packed her trunk for the honeymoon?' She fell about again.

The Doctor stood, arms crossed, looking at her with a stony face that made her laugh even more. 'Got that out of your system?'

She nodded, still sniggering.

'Then can we get on with stopping time and space from ripping apart? We can? Then *let's get on with it.*'

Rose composed herself and raised her hands in a 'what?' gesture.

'Right. You're Fortuna, you hide behind the statue, you don't, repeat don't, let me see you, and you wait until Gracilis has picked up the phial and left before you come out again. Oh, and take this – it'll disguise your voice. OK?' He handed her a small metal device and hustled her towards the door. 'Go go go!'

'Hang on,' said Rose, trying to dig in her heels. 'Can't I have a rehearsal or something?'

The Doctor glanced at the scanner. 'No time! I'm going to be here any second! Oh, and Rose –'

She turned back. 'Mm?'

'Yeah, I'm afraid she had. Packed her trunk. And said goodbye to the circus.' He gave her a big grin – and propelled her through the doors.

Rose found herself stumbling out into the shrine, and the

TARDIS doors slammed behind her. The time machine was soon swallowed up in the gloom as she made her way to the statue that the Doctor had indicated. It was a bit of a squeeze to get behind and she could only hope that the gloom would disguise her too; she felt that bits of her were sticking out all over the place.

She had just settled down and adjusted the metal box thing over her mouth, when the door to the shrine opened. She peered through Fortuna's legs and saw that, yes, it was the Doctor. He saw the statue. She shrank back as he hurried forward... and then he realised that it wasn't her.

Rose was taken aback. She hadn't known – how could she know? – what her disappearance had done to him. This Doctor had a look of such despair in his eyes that her heart almost stopped in pity. She wanted more than anything else in the world to jump up, go to him, tell him that everything was going to be all right.

But, what with possibly ripping time and space apart, that was probably a bad idea.

'Rose is prettier than you,' the Doctor suddenly said.

'Thanks!' she said, before she could stop herself. She bit her tongue. Quick, better follow on with the rest of it before he got too suspicious. The box over her mouth made her sound more like Cher than Rose, but she put on her best 'goddess' voice anyway and said, 'This'll bring Rose back to life – and the others. All praise to me – that is, Fortuna,' she hastily clarified, 'and all that.'

She bent down as low as she could, and carefully – oh, so carefully – sent the little glass phial on its journey towards the Doctor, and her past.

The Doctor picked it up and started towards her. She tensed up, suddenly wondering if he would discover her after all – but, just as the Doctor had described, he was interrupted by Gracilis.

Rose couldn't bear to watch the Doctor's capture, even though she knew it had a happy ending. She forced herself to look at the moment when he dropped the phial, though. That was important. Now she just had to wait for Gracilis to pick it up…

Gracilis wrung his hands in despair. 'What do I do? What do I do?' she heard him mutter to himself. 'I must find someone who can help.'

The old man walked towards the exit. Any moment now…

Gracilis passed the phial. Rose waited for him to spot it and stop – but he didn't.

He opened the doors. He walked outside…

Rose felt a swirling, sinking feeling in her stomach, and she didn't know if it was fear or if history really had just changed and she was about to be erased from existence. If Gracilis had never found the phial…

And then she had an idea. Whether it was sensible or not she hadn't time to decide – probably it wasn't. But what she said, hoping that the GENIE was close enough to hear her, was, 'I wish Gracilis would come back now and find the phial.'

There was a crash of thunder inside her head.

And Gracilis walked back through the door. He was shaking his head, frowning as if trying to place something. He looked at the ground. Aha! He picked up the phial of life-giving liquid and put it in a pouch at his waist.

Rose heaved a very big sigh of relief.

EIGHTEEN

'That would be the end of the adventure, then,' Rose said to the Doctor, as the TARDIS took off again. 'Everything's going to happen when it should. Old you'll get the phial of liquid and bring everyone back and then give the empty phial to me to get filled again to give to you and it all works.'

'Thank goodness!' said Vanessa.

She'd been trying to help the Doctor determine the exact time and place to which she should be returned. She turned to Rose, as if it was already goodbye. 'Thank you – for everything.'

'That's all right,' said Rose. 'Just – be careful what you wish for in future, OK?'

Vanessa grinned.

The TARDIS landed and Rose opened the doors. Vanessa hurried out, eager to be home. The Doctor and Rose followed her more slowly.

They'd arrived in a small study. The TARDIS stood on a beautiful Persian-style rug and silk draperies hung across the walls. A screen was showing a documentary. 'This was the Golden Age of Rome...' the voiceover was saying.

'Power's back, then,' said the Doctor.

He glanced over to one side. On a desk a faint square mark could just be made out in the light coating of dust – where a cardboard box may once have stood.

'Father doesn't like being disturbed by the robocleaners,' Vanessa explained, slightly embarrassed.

'I don't blame him,' said the Doctor. 'And talking of your father… His research is going to be destroyed and so is his laboratory. But his brain will still work. Whatever you do, you mustn't let him build another GENIE. Fate of the world, Vanessa. Fate – of – the – world.' He sketched a wave.

'Er… yeah,' said Rose, not sure how to follow that. 'Take care of yourself, OK?'

They went back into the TARDIS, leaving a very worried-looking girl behind them.

The TARDIS doors had shut and they were in flight again.

'The question now,' said the Doctor, 'is what we're going to do with you.' He was looking at the GENIE. 'You're a bit dangerous, you know? Even if all the kinks had been ironed out, no offence.'

The creature looked troubled, and Rose's heart was suddenly touched. Yeah, it had caused some bother – the whole being-turned-to-stone thing for a start. But that hadn't been the GENIE's fault – like the Doctor had said before, it was people who were to blame.

'I've got an idea,' she said.

'I'm all ears,' said the Doctor.

Rose dug him in the ribs. 'Not so much any more!'

'Your idea, Miss Tyler?' he said with a mock frown.

'Right. Well, I was just thinking about what you said ages ago,' she told him.

'If I said it, it must have been good. What did I say?'

'About slaves,' she said. 'About how they can buy their freedom – or be freed. And the GENIE – well, in the stories, isn't he sometimes called the Slave of the Lamp? I know all about Aladdin. Well, I've seen the Disney film anyway. Which is brilliant, by the way. Robin Williams, he's so funny, and – Yeah, right,' she added quickly after a glance from the Doctor. 'Anyway, the point is – the GENIE can't wish for itself. But I can wish for it – like how I got it to turn into a monkey. And Aladdin's last wish is to free the genie. To make it so it doesn't have to grant wishes any more. So it isn't a slave. I could do that.'

The GENIE looked dismayed. 'But granting wishes is what I was built for! It's all I've ever known!'

Rose shook her head. 'Don't you see? You could still grant wishes, if you wanted to. But it'd be your choice. You wouldn't have to do things that would destroy people, or hurt them, or anything like that.'

'My… choice?' said the GENIE.

'Yeah!'

'That is… freedom?'

'That's freedom.'

'Then perhaps… I should like it,' said the GENIE. 'I should like freedom.'

Rose took a deep breath. 'Here goes, then.' She glanced at the Doctor, who nodded approval. 'I wish… that the GENIE is free. That it doesn't have to grant wishes unless it wants to. That it's not a slave any more.'

A ray of light shot from the console and hit the GENIE, which seemed to suck it in like spaghetti. There was a peal of thunder; a triumphant crash.

'Has anything changed?' said Rose.

'Why not try it and see?' the Doctor suggested.

'I wish…' said Rose, thinking, 'I wish… that the Doctor's nose was green.'

'Hey!' he said.

Rose opened her eyes wide in horror. 'Oh, no! Looks like the GENIE isn't free after all…'

The Doctor ran off to get a mirror, and Rose collapsed with laughter. 'Freedom OK for you, then?' she asked the GENIE.

The little creature drew itself up to its full height – which wasn't that much, but suddenly seemed to convey a dignity that hadn't been there before. 'Freedom is indeed… OK,' it said.

Rose crouched down beside it. 'You know, you don't have to grant wishes any more. But if there was anything you wanted granted for yourself, you know – I could help out.'

The GENIE reached out a tiny scaly paw. 'I should like,' it said, 'to go somewhere… nice. A place where there are no people to covet my power. A simple place. A place where I can be… happy.' A tear slipped from its eye and dripped off the end of its beak.

'Then I wish that for you,' said Rose.

Crash!

And the GENIE disappeared.

But Rose thought she heard the words 'thank you' echo through the air as it did so.

'So,' said Rose, 'that really is the end of the adventure this time. And we never have to go back to Rome ag—' She suddenly gasped and dived at the console. She began hitting buttons at random. 'We've got to go back! We've got to go back and undo everything!'

The Doctor opened his eyes wide. 'We have?'

'Yes!' She stared at him, urging him to realise the importance of this. 'Don't you see? Ursus never made that statue – the statue in the museum! We've got to go back and get him to make it somehow, or when we go back to the twenty-first century reality will explode!'

'Well, we wouldn't want that.' The Doctor was laughing as he gently removed her hands from the controls.

'Don't you be so condescending!' she said angrily. 'Laugh all you like, I'm trying to save the world!'

He stopped laughing, but he didn't seem able to stop grinning. 'I'm not laughing at you,' he said. 'Actually we do need to pop back to Rome, but not for that reason. Come on.'

He took her by the hand and led her out of the control room and into a little side room. There, amid a lot of sculpting paraphernalia, was her statue. The statue from the museum. The statue of Fortuna. New and gleaming.

Rose gaped. 'But I never posed for this.'

'No need,' said the Doctor, patting it on the arm – an arm which still had a hand attached.

'What d'you mean?'

'I mean,' he explained, 'that you won't have to pose for it. As Mickey said –' the Doctor smiled to himself – 'it was sculpted by someone who knew you pretty well.'

He ran a hand through his hair and looked as though he was expecting applause.

Rose walked round the statue. 'Is my bum really that—'

'Yes,' the Doctor interrupted testily. 'This statue is accurate in every detail. Bum. Arms. Legs. Nose. Broken fingernail on your right hand.'

Rose looked down. 'Hey, even I hadn't noticed that!

Well?'

'Well what?'

'Well, where did it come from?'

He sighed exasperatedly. 'I made it.'

Rose laughed. 'No, really.'

'Yes, really.'

'What, you're serious? But, like, how? I didn't know you sculpted. You said you didn't sculpt. You said you weren't a master sculptor. I heard you.'

'I learned,' the Doctor said.

She was puzzled. 'When?'

'This is a time machine,' he said – and told her everything. How he lost her trail. How he went back to the British Museum. How he realised the truth.

'The earrings gave me the first clue,' he said. 'But when Mickey and I turned her over and found my signature on the bottom –'

'You'd better not have signed my bottom,' said Rose.

'– on the base,' continued the Doctor, 'well, that was a bit of a hint too.'

'You mean to say no one had ever noticed that this statue had got "the Doctor" written on it before?' asked Rose. "Cause wouldn't they have wondered why?'

'Ah,' said the Doctor. 'Gallifreyan signature. They'd have no idea what it was. Anyway, then I knew I had to find the real you – and find a sculpture to take your place. I did think for a minute about just nicking that statue and bringing it back here, but well – then it would have been a 4,000-year-old statue, which would not only have confused people but also set up all sorts of paradoxes, and I think we've had enough of those for the moment. Better not to risk the whole of causality if you don't have to. So, anyway, quick flick of the coordinates, back to the Renaissance, took that sculpting course.' He produced Rose's mobile. 'Mickey texted me pictures so I got it just right, and Michelangelo helped with the tricky bits. Like your ears, they were a nightmare to get right. And then, when it was all finished, I came back to Rome a couple of days before I left, and hid outside Gracilis's place, ready to follow Ursus when he went off with… with you. Rescue effected, all's right with the world.'

Rose was almost speechless for a moment. 'You went gallivanting off for months and months with *Michelangelo* while I was left standing there like something a dog might put its leg up against?'

'You were only stone for a couple of hours!' said the Doctor indignantly. 'And it was your idea in the first place. Sort of. A bit. And you wouldn't believe what a slave-driver Michelangelo is. Everything has to be perfect.'

Rose stood looking at the statue for a bit longer. 'It is perfect,' she said at last.

'I was inspired.'

They smiled at each other. All was right with the world again.

'Anyway,' the Doctor continued, 'you know what? I think you bring me luck. My Fortuna, that's you.'

'You mean I'm a sort of mascot,' said Rose. 'Like a four-leaf clover. Or wearing lucky pants when you go for an interview.'

'That's it exactly,' the Doctor told her. 'You're my lucky pants.' Then he said, more seriously, 'I realised it when you pretended to be Fortuna in that shrine. Knew it was right to portray you like that.'

Rose frowned. 'But you only went to that shrine because

you'd already seen the statue of me as Fortuna.'

'And there was only that statue of Fortuna because I'd seen what a good Fortuna you'd make.'

'Another paradox?'

The Doctor grinned. 'Only the tiniest of tiny ones. More like circular logic. Like how no one ever actually came up with that very complicated formula to turn people back from stone.'

'So they didn't!' Rose realised. Then she thought of something else. 'You said that Fortuna's sometimes got a blindfold on. So she doesn't know who she favours.'

He nodded.

'So sometimes she turns her back on people who've relied on her. Sometimes the luck… goes away.'

'And lucky pants are just pants, and four-leaf clovers are just vegetation, and a rabbit's foot just means you should call the RSPCA. I'll survive.'

Rose helped the Doctor carry the statue into the control room. It glowed like green jade in the light from the central column.

'It doesn't look half bad in here, don't you think? Sort of goes with the decor.'

'I think one Rose per TARDIS is quite enough,' said the Doctor, who was now bent over the console. 'Some might say too much.'

She pouted.

'Anyway, you know it can't stay here. We've got to find it a new home.'

The TARDIS landed and Rose stepped out nervously. But she knew where they were at once. 'We're back at the villa!'

she said as the Doctor joined her.

'Yup,' he said. 'Thought you might fancy a Roman holiday.'

She glared at him.

'Or maybe not. Come on. Job to do.'

A slave spotted them and ran into the villa. Seconds later, Gracilis and Marcia ran out, followed by a boy Rose had never seen before – at least not like this. But she knew who he was.

'You must be Optatus,' she said, grinning at him.

He nodded shyly. 'And you are Rose. I must thank you for all you have done for me.'

She tried to look modest. 'Oh, it was nothing really.'

Marcia swept her up in a hug. 'You say it is nothing! What you and the Doctor have done for us can never be repaid! Oh, I feared for your safety – we have not seen you since… since…'

'Oh, don't worry about that,' said Rose hastily, realising that their last GENIE-orchestrated meeting would be – at least, she hoped it would be – a bit of a blur.

But Marcia was still frowning. 'You – and the slave Vanessa…'

'Ah!' The Doctor put an arm round Gracilis's shoulder. 'Now, I wanted to have a word with you about her.'

'Indeed?' said Gracilis.

'Indeed indeed. The thing is, I know she belongs to you.'

Rose snorted, and the Doctor threw her a look.

'I know she belongs to you. But she isn't coming back.'

Gracilis opened his mouth to speak, but the Doctor shushed him.

'I know you paid a lot of money for her. But look at it this way. You bought her to help get your son back – and you've got your son back. You don't need any more slaves. You've just taken on another couple of dozen. And… I'd like to give you something in exchange for her freedom. If I could just borrow a bit of muscle…'

With the aid of some slaves, the Doctor brought the Fortuna statue out of the TARDIS and it was carried over to Gracilis.

'I thought you might have a spare spot for this,' the Doctor said. 'After all, you're missing a statue now…'

So the stone Rose was taken to the little grove just outside the villa entrance.

'Careful!' called Gracilis, as the statue knocked hard against a wall during an awkward turn.

'Is it OK?' asked Rose.

'Oh, yes,' said the Doctor. 'Well, maybe there's a slight crack. Just at the wrist.' And he grinned.

The Doctor and Rose sat in the grove. The sun sparkled across the pond, throwing glitterball reflections across the white marble of the statue. The Doctor petted a peacock, which made a mewing noise like a cat. He mewed back at it.

They'd been sitting alone for a while when Gracilis joined them again. He begged their pardon, but he wanted to ask them something.

'That girl, Vanessa,' he said. 'She was a true reader of the stars, wasn't she?'

Rose wasn't sure what to say, but the Doctor nodded. 'I suppose you could say that.'

Gracilis was quiet for a moment, thinking. Then he continued, 'I think she was sent by the gods to aid us. And I think you too were sent by the gods.'

Rose laughed. 'No, really, we weren't. Honest.'

'In that case,' Gracilis said, looking at the statue, 'you must be gods yourselves.'

'No, we're not!' Rose began, but Gracilis had risen and was moving off.

'I will honour you all my life,' he said.

'Gracilis!'

Rose had suddenly thought of something.

He stopped and turned back. 'Yes, my lady?'

'Just – no sacrifices, OK?'

Gracilis smiled and bowed.

Rose took a last look at her statue as they stood up, ready to head back to the TARDIS and places new.

Almost 1,900 years later, a grainy picture of that same statue was sellotaped to a cupboard in Jackie Tyler's kitchen. It was a shame they didn't do a proper postcard of it, but Mickey had taken a photo on his phone and had it blown up for her, and that was better than nothing. Her daughter. Her beautiful daughter, Rose. Jackie started singing to herself as she opened the cupboard to get out a microwave meal for one.

In the British Museum, Mickey Smith was standing in the sculpture room. 'This is the goddess Fortuna,' he said to the group of kids he was taking round. 'She brought luck – or took it away. But you'd put up with whatever she did. Because when she decided to favour you, it made everything worthwhile.'

And the kids, who'd been fidgeting and punching each other and daring each other to nick stuff from the gift shop, heard something in his voice that actually made them pay attention for a moment.

'She's pretty,' said one of the kids.

'Ha! She's your girlfriend!' one of the others retorted. 'You love her!'

And Mickey grinned as he led the taunting, teasing kids to the next exhibit.

Nearly 370 years after that, Vanessa Moretti spent another lonely day in the house, while her father was off supervising the building of his new laboratory. She thought back longingly to the time she'd spent in Rome. How could she have hated it so much? Surely anywhere was better than here. Mind you, it all seemed like a dream now. She remembered the Doctor telling her a long story, something about her father. But now she was home, she couldn't seem to remember it. She wished she could see the Doctor and Rose again, ask them about it.

But she didn't have the GENIE any more, so wishes didn't come true just like that.

She wished she did have a GENIE.

Perhaps her father would be able to build another one.

And who knew how far in space or time from there, a little scaly creature with the claws of a dragon and the beak of a duck sat admiring its surroundings. The grass was green and the sun shone. An animal resembling a large guinea pig wandered over to the newcomer and examined it with interest.

The GENIE looked at the guinea pig. 'Ah, my furry friend,' it said, 'if you had a wish, what would you wish for?'

The guinea pig squeaked. There was the sound of thunder rumbling and then an orange, carrot-like vegetable appeared. The guinea pig squeaked again.

'You're welcome,' said the GENIE. Despite its beak, it almost seemed to be smiling. 'I think I shall be happy here.'

ACKNOWLEDGEMENTS

Thanks to many people:

Helen Raynor, queen of script editors, for help and advice; and Russell T Davies, without whom…

Justin for always being there, and being such a damn fine editor too; and, together with Steve, without whom writing these books wouldn't be anywhere near as much fun;

Lesley, for help and insight;

Phil Cole, fellow one-time Nottingham classicist, for historical reassurance;

David Bailey and Mark Wright for being jolly helpful – and jolly in general;

and of course Mum, Dad and Helen, Jan, Chris and Marie, and my wonderful husband, Nick, for their love and support.

Also available in the Doctor Who *History Collection:*

THE ROUNDHEADS

MARK GATISS

ISBN 978 1 849 90903 7

With the Civil War won, the Parliamentarians are struggling to hang on to power. But plans are being made to rescue the defeated King Charles from his prison...

With Ben press-ganged and put on board a mysterious ship bound for Amsterdam, Polly becomes an unwitting accomplice in the plot to rescue the King. The Doctor can't help because he and Jamie have been arrested and sent to the Tower of London, charged with conspiracy.

Can the Doctor and Jamie escape, find Ben and rescue Polly – while making sure that history remains on its proper course?

An adventure set in the aftermath of the English Civil War, featuring the Second Doctor, as played by Patrick Troughton, and his companions Ben, Polly and Jamie.

Also available in the Doctor Who *History Collection:*

The Witch Hunters

Steve Lyons

ISBN 978 1 849 90902 0

With the Doctor wanting to repair the TARDIS in peace and quiet, Barbara, Ian and Susan decide to get some experience of living in the nearby village of Salem. But the Doctor knows about the horrors destined to engulf the village and determines that they should leave.

His friends are not impressed. His granddaughter Susan has her own ideas, and is desperate to return, whatever the cost. But perhaps the Doctor was right. Perhaps Susan's actions will lead them all into terrible danger and cause the tragedy that is already unfolding to escalate out of control.

An adventure set during the seventeenth-century Salem Witch Trials, featuring the First Doctor, as played by William Hartnell, and his companions Susan, Ian and Barbara.

Also available in the Doctor Who *History Collection:*

Dead of Winter

James Goss

ISBN 978 1 849 90907 5

In a remote clinic in eighteenth-century Italy, a lonely girl writes to her mother. She tells of pale English aristocrats and mysterious Russian nobles. She tells of intrigues and secrets, and strange faceless figures that rise up from the sea. And she tells about the enigmatic Mrs Pond, who arrives with her husband and her trusted physician.

What the girl doesn't tell her mother is the truth that everyone at the clinic knows and no one says – that the only people who come here do so to die.

An adventure set in eighteenth-century Italy, featuring the Eleventh Doctor, as played by Matt Smith, and his companions Amy and Rory.

Also available in the Doctor Who *History Collection:*

HUMAN NATURE

PAUL CORNELL

ISBN 978 1 849 90909 9

Hulton College in Norfolk is a school dedicated to producing military officers. With the First World War about to start, the boys of the school will soon be on the front line. But no one expects a war – not even Dr John Smith, the college's new house master…

The Doctor's friend Benny is enjoying her holiday in the same town. But then she meets a future version of the Doctor, and things start to get dangerous very quickly. With the Doctor she knows gone, and only a suffragette and an elderly rake for company, can Benny fight off a vicious alien attack? And will Dr Smith be able to save the day?

An adventure set in Britain on the eve of the First World War, featuring the Seventh Doctor, as played by Sylvester McCoy, and his companion Bernice Summerfield. This book was the basis for the Tenth Doctor television story Human Nature / The Family of Blood *starring David Tennant.*

Also available in the Doctor Who *History Collection:*

THE ENGLISH WAY OF DEATH

GARETH ROBERTS

ISBN 978 1 849 90908 2

The Doctor, Romana and K-9 are hoping for a holiday in London in the sweltering summer of 1930. But the TARDIS is warning of time pollution. And that's not the only problem.

What connects the isolated Sussex resort of Nutchurch with the secret society run by the eccentric Percy Closed? Why has millionaire Hepworth Stackhouse dismissed his staff and hired assassin Julia Orlostro? And what is the truth behind the infernal vapour known only as Zodaal?

With the heat building, the Doctor and his friends set out to solve the mysteries.

An adventure set in 1930s London, featuring the Fourth Doctor, as played by Tom Baker, and his companions Romana and K-9.

Also available in the Doctor Who *History Collection:*

THE SHADOW IN THE GLASS

JUSTIN RICHARDS AND STEPHEN COLE

ISBN 978 1 849 90905 1

When a squadron of RAF Hurricanes shoots down an unidentified aircraft over Turelhampton, the village is immediately evacuated. But why is the village still guarded by troops in 2001? When a television documentary crew break through the cordon looking for a story, they find they've recorded more than they'd bargained for.

Caught up in both a deadly conspiracy and a historical mystery, retired Brigadier Lethbridge-Stewart calls upon his old friend the Doctor. Half-glimpsed demons watch from the shadows as the Doctor and the Brigadier travel back in time to discover the last, and deadliest, secret of the Second World War.

An adventure set partly in the Second Wold War, featuring the Sixth Doctor, as played by Colin Baker, and Brigadier Lethbridge-Stewart.